THE BLAZING GLEN

Handsome Englishman Alastair Fenton is met with hostility when he first encounters Janet Mackay in Sutherland. However, when Janet and her grandmother, Mary, are evicted from their croft, and then Mary dies, Alastair protects Janet on the journey to Glasgow. Janet's plans to join her brother in Canada are shattered when all her money is stolen. Murdo, her childhood sweetheart, helps her get a job, but his constant urgings that they marry begin to irk Janet, as do Alastair's repeated offers to look after her.

LIVVY WEST

◆

THE BLAZING GLEN

Complete and Unabridged

LINFORD
Leicester

First published in Great Britain in 2004

First Linford Edition
published 2005

British Library CIP Data

West, Livvy
The blazing glen.—Large print ed.—
Linford romance library
1. Eviction—Scotland—Highlands—Fiction
2. Love stories 3. Large type books
I. Title
823.9'14 [F]

ISBN 1–84395–594–6

Published by
F. A. Thorpe (Publishing)
Anstey, Leicestershire

Set by Words & Graphics Ltd.
Anstey, Leicestershire
Printed and bound in Great Britain by
T. J. International Ltd., Padstow, Cornwall

This book is printed on acid-free paper

1

She saw him coming from a great distance, the air was so clear. A gentle breeze blew in from the sea some miles away, bringing with it a faint tang of salt and fish. The path from the south was in full view as it descended the gentle slope.

The turf, with morning dew long dried, shone with new growth, a pale bright green in the sunlight, then black as the slope rose into the rocky shadows of Ben Kilbreck, silhouetted against a pale blue sky.

Automatically Janet assessed the few fluffy clouds, and decided there would be no storms today. Since living here she'd become aware of the weather as never before.

The stranger was riding a good horse, a bright chestnut which stood out against the grass, far superior to the few rough-coated ponies the local people had for their needs. He would no doubt be visiting a minister, or a tacksman farther along the Strathnaver. No-one else of wealth or importance lived in this part of Sutherland.

She turned away, losing interest in someone who could have no business with her, or any of the crofters in the small township down by the loch. Slowly, she moved farther up the hillside, searching for the herbs and plants she needed, ingredients to ease the aches in her grandmother's crippled joints and wasted, twisted body.

'Your pardon, mistress.'

The soft, southern voice made her start in alarm and almost drop the basket into which she was placing the herbs. She'd heard no sound of his approach.

'What do you want?'

Surprise, and a quiver of alarm, made her curt as she turned to face him. They saw few strangers here, and those who had come of late had been unwelcome.

He'd left his horse tethered to a spindly tree lower down the slope, and his soft, leather boots had made no sound on the springy turf.

'I frightened you. I'm sorry. I'm heading for Syre, but it's so long since I saw any habitations I thought I was lost. It's a vast country, and lonely. I tried to take a short cut, but am afraid I may have missed the way. My name's Alastair Fenton. Am I in the right way?'

'I'm Janet Mackay,' she replied automatically, and brushed the strands of hair which had escaped from beneath her kerchief out of her eyes.

He was tall, more so than her brother, Iain, who had been tall even for a Highlander. Where was Iain now? It was months since they'd heard from him, apart from that one brief letter, and months before that since he'd had to flee the glen. At least he'd been safe when he wrote that.

'Well, Janet Mackay, am I riding in the right direction? Are you unwilling, or unable to help the benighted traveller?' his voice interrupted her thoughts.

She shook her head to clear it of thoughts of Iain, for dwelling on his fate served no purpose, and concentrated on the stranger. He had dark brown hair with a lighter hint. His clothes were of good quality, rich materials, not the homespun most men wore, and excellently tailored. He looked Scottish, somehow, but his name and his voice were English. What was he doing here? She'd come to fear and distrust the English even more in the past few months.

'You can follow the loch and then the river, and Syre's no more than an hour's ride,' she said abruptly, pointing to where the waters of the loch gleamed dark and mysterious.

He smiled, and she took a step backwards. He was handsome, she realised suddenly, with his dark, deep-set eyes, and regular features, and his smile seemed to show he was fully, even arrogantly aware of it.

His cravat was a brilliant white, starched and folded to perfection. The dark blue riding coat did little to disguise his athletic figure, and his breeches were close-fitting, his legs long and muscular.

She swallowed. She'd never seen such a handsome man, so smooth-faced, clean-shaven and fine-skinned. He was tanned, but not like the men of the glen who had complexions weathered by the sun and the wind, hands roughened by hard work, and often beards to help keep out the cold of the Highland winters.

Apart from that tan he reminded her of the men she'd once known in Edinburgh. They'd had no idea what it meant to carve an existence out of harsh, unforgiving land, men who lived soft lives, spent their time in gaming and frivolity, and expected others to serve them and provide for their every need.

'You live nearby? I see no houses,' he said, and Janet, though she knew this hillside as well as she'd known her father's garden, glanced round as if to look for what she knew could not be there.

The hillside was deserted of people other than the two of them. There were just a few black cattle grazing on the lower slopes, and some sheep and goats.

'I live down by the loch,' she told him briefly. 'The houses are hidden amongst those trees.'

'You needn't fear me,' he said softly.

Janet gasped. She hadn't been aware of her tenseness, her clenched hands and the fluttering of butterflies in her stomach until he mentioned fear, but suddenly she knew that she was wary of him.

There was no other soul within sight or hearing, and he had such a confident air about him.

'Why should I fear you?' she demanded angrily, and turned abruptly away. 'I bid you farewell, Mr Fenton,' she said over her shoulder, the training of her governesses forcing her to be polite.

He laughed.

'No reason. Please, sit for a while with me and tell me about yourself, how the people here live. Though my mother comes from Scotland, I live in England, near a town called Stafford, and it's my first time so far north.'

She knew then why he was here, and the knowledge did nothing to comfort her. Instead she was consumed with a bitter rage. There had been other English visitors, lured by the thought of vast acres to rent, and fortunes to be made from populating the hills with sheep, while driving out the people who had lived and farmed here for centuries.

'So you want our land?' she demanded furiously. 'The land we've tended for generations past! You, from Stafford, where the marquis who married our countess has his English estates, are not content with what you have in England. You must ruin us, too!'

'Wait,' he snapped, and, reaching out, grasped her arm before she thought to move out of reach. 'I'm not looking to ruin anyone.'

'Let me go!'

She struggled to free herself but his grasp tightened.

'Listen to me, will you?'

'Why are you here?' she gasped.

'I'm not your enemy,' he began, but she shook her head and impetuously interrupted him.

'I said let me go! All the Englishmen who come here are wanting only to drive us away. I don't want to listen to your excuses.'

'Just like a woman, always talking and never listening. But you will,' he said, and laughed.

His eyes glinted with amusement, and Janet renewed her struggles to be free of his grasp. As well as attacking her he was mocking her, which made her even more angry.

'I'll have to change that,' he went on. 'This is a confounded nuisance,' he added lightly, and calmly removed the basket from her hand to set it down behind him.

Then he laid a hand on her lips. That infuriated Janet still more, but before she could reply she became tinglingly aware that he was pulling her closer towards him.

She bit his fingers, tried to kick him, and began to struggle in earnest. Freeing one hand for a moment, she swung her arm back and dealt him a stinging slap on the cheek.

He paused, startled, and then his expression hardened. She didn't like the gleam she saw in his eyes. It no longer indicated simple amusement, but promised retribution, and something more she couldn't interpret. Fear and fury struggled for supremacy in her mind.

'Wild cat!' he hissed. 'Your temper certainly matches that dark, fiery hair of yours!'

He pulled her closer still, and managed to imprison both her arms so that she was powerless to move away.

She breathed deeply and twisted aside. His hand came up and dragged off the kerchief she had tied round her head. Her long hair, unbound, fell over his hand and down her back.

'Silky, and as lovely as your face,' he murmured, stroking it, and then, as she took a deep breath and opened her mouth to scream, even though she knew it was useless, his mouth came down to cover hers and silenced her.

It seemed hours before he lifted his head, and she was able to draw in a shuddering breath. When he spoke, his tone had changed. Now it was gentle, not angry.

'And they always say green eyes mean passion.'

He let her go and Janet moved away unsteadily, wiping her lips with the back of her hand. They were bruised, and she felt as though her bones had liquefied.

She wanted to run, but knew she'd collapse within yards. How dare he treat her so!

She hated all Englishmen, for the

misery and devastation they'd brought to the Highlands after Culloden, killing so many people and causing the lairds to lose hope, and neglect their kinsfolk. Her own grandfather had been killed then, nearly seventy years ago.

He'd left his young and pregnant wife to scrape a living as best she could, with the child who'd been born sickly. Her father had only survived because of her grandmother's skill with medicines, a skill she was now teaching Janet.

And still it went on. Their own Countess Elizabeth's English husband, the Marquess of Stafford, was turning people off the land they'd farmed for generations past recall. Soon it would be their turn, for they'd received notices to quit by May.

That was just a couple of weeks away and Janet was dreading the time coming. She doubted if her grandmother, old and ill, could endure the lengthy journey to Thurso. At least she had somewhere to go if she survived the journey. Her sister was willing to take her in.

Now she had a focus for her hatred — this arrogant Englishman who came and treated her like a common tavern wench. To her relief, for she had no strength to resist him, he turned away and took a few hasty steps away from her.

'I can't say I'm sorry,' he said, and gave a snort of laughter. 'It was a delightful experience, but if I am to resist further temptation I had best be on my way. Goodbye, dear Janet.'

She sank on to the ground, trembling, and watched as he strode down the hill, collected his horse, vaulted into the saddle, and kicked the animal into a canter.

She'd been kissed before. Murdo Mackay, a distant cousin who lived farther along the glen in the next township, had been paying her special attention ever since she came here three years ago, when she was only sixteen.

Devastated by the deaths, within a

few days of each other, of her parents, she had turned to the only other young person around, apart from her brother, and Murdo had now assumed they would marry soon. She'd accepted his kisses at first, but they had been nothing like that bruising, searing, astonishing kiss from the unknown Englishman.

Her lips still felt warm, and she ran her tongue over them slowly, then touched them with her fingers. Why had he done it? And why had she permitted it? It was no good telling herself that she'd had little choice, or been too shocked to move. She could have struggled more.

She wished she'd been able to reach the dirk she carried at her girdle. Then she'd have shown him how unwise it was to take from her what she had no wish to give. But she'd been unable to resist, and she wondered, feeling a wave of embarrassed shame, if she'd truly wanted to resist.

Had she really not wished to have

that kiss, once the initial shock of it was over?

It did no good to brood. She stood up and collected her basket, from which, miraculously, she had dropped none of the herbs.

Though she kept a better look-out than she'd been doing before, she was nervous for the rest of the time she spent on the hillside. When she was ready to go back to the croft and milk their cow, she felt a strange sense of relief.

Her grandmother, old Mary, was sitting on the bench outside the croft, enjoying the spring sunshine which, she said, warmed her bones.

'You look hot,' she said, peering up at Janet, and Janet nodded, trying to behave normally.

'It is a hot day,' she agreed, and went into the small cottage, just the two rooms with the byre at one end.

She sorted the herbs, hanging them to dry in bunches from the roof trusses, then picked up the milking pail. Though her grandmother always rejected any suggestion that she had second sight, she was uncannily perceptive, and for some reason Janet had no wish to mention the encounter with the Englishman, not even just to report his presence. One stranger more or less made no difference to them.

She couldn't forget him, though.

Throughout that night she lay sleepless, trying not to disturb her grandmother. Her thoughts drifted to her father. He'd been taught well by the local minister, and had gone to make his fortune in Edinburgh. It hadn't been easy, but he'd become a man of business, and at the age of forty, rich and respected, he'd taken a wife.

Iain had been born a year later, but they had given up hope of more children for several years before Janet had been born. He'd wanted his mother, Mary, to join them in Edinburgh, but she had refused, saying she could not endure the thought of living in a town.

'You'll soon be able to follow Iain, my love,' Mary's voice suddenly came out of the darkness. 'I've not long to wait before I join my own Jamie.'

'You're to stay with me as long as you can,' Janet said fiercely. 'I don't want to lose you, too. We've the cart and pony, and when the weather is warmer, we'll get to Thurso.'

'I'm well over eighty, and that's a good age. I'm ready to go. My one regret will be leaving you, lass, but I'd rather die here where I was once happy than in a strange bed.'

'Well, I'm not ready to let you! Why, old Donald at Rossal is one hundred.'

Mary chuckled.

'And look at the life he leads, never able to leave his bed. I can still hobble outside to the bench to sit in the sun, but do you think I'd want to stay on if even that was denied me? I don't want to leave you, but you'll be better off with Iain in Nova Scotia.'

She fell silent, and soon Janet was certain she was asleep. Her thoughts drifted to her brother. At least he'd survived the difficult journey, they had that to be thankful for. So many did not.

They'd had one letter sent from Halifax, written after the voyage, to say he was travelling farther, to Montreal, with other emigrants who'd been forced to leave their own land and seek a new life far away across the sea. He'd told her of a man she could contact in Halifax, who would be able to tell her where he was.

She would follow him when Mary died. That had been agreed, and he had left money for her passage, a purse with enough gold to keep her until she could rejoin him. He'd needed the rest of their father's fortune to buy good land in Canada.

Mary had wanted her to go with Iain, but she had insisted she preferred to remain and look after the frail, old woman.

Her emotions were so tangled. She dreaded the inevitable death of the old lady who'd become so close to her during the last few years, taking the place of both mother and father, and then, when Iain had been forced to flee, of him, too. She was all the family they had left, but it was true, she had not many more years to live, and then Janet, too, would face the hazardous crossing of the seas to follow her brother.

Life in Canada was hard, she'd heard, but at least they could hope to prosper from hard work, and not, as here in Scotland, lose it all on the whim of the lairds.

She was milking the cow early the next morning, leaning her head against the soft, warm flank and trying to stifle her yawns, when Murdo strode into the byre.

'What's this about you and that Englishman?' he demanded.

'Englishman?' Janet asked, surprised.

'Aye, a painted popinjay who's never done an honest day's work in his life, and who's having the nerve to ask about you, who you are, where you live, your age, your family. He's one of Sellar's men, no doubt, looking at the land they've leased, our land by right! When did ye meet him?'

'Murdo, I don't know what you're talking about!' Janet said, her heart beating so loudly she thought he must hear it.

'Did ye meet a dratted Englishman yesterday?' he demanded.

'A man asked me the way, but what's that to be making such a fuss? And what if he was English? He was probably looking to find some land to rent, but there's none here. Patrick Sellar has it all, and he's the factor. He decides who rents it from him.'

If she hoped to distract Murdo she did not succeed. His face, already ruddy from exposure to the weather, turned a darker red.

'If all he did was ask the way, and all you did was tell him, why should he be so interested in you?'

'How can I prevent a strange traveller

from saying what he wishes?' Janet demanded, exasperated. 'Now let me finish here. Go and say good morning to Mary.'

Glowering, he swung on his heel and left, but not to visit Mary. Instead, he strode farther along the narrow track which wound between the small cottages.

When Janet came out of the byre carrying the pail of milk, she saw him talking earnestly to another young man, one of the band who'd grown up together, who now drank together, and often talked wildly of what they'd like to do to the English.

They turned and looked at her, but she ignored them. She had butter to churn, a hare one of their neighbours had caught to skin and clean for their supper, and bread to make. She had no time for idle speculation.

Her tasks, however, many as they were, did not fill her mind. Time and again her thoughts turned to the previous day, that strange encounter, the kiss which had been so unwelcome, and yet in a way so exciting.

Why had the handsome Englishman come here? And would she ever see him again?

2

A couple of days later, Janet was returning from the lochside with two pails of water when she heard children giggling. They were hiding behind a clump of bushes at the end of the path, where it joined the main track through the village. She smiled. They had few worries, no fears for the future when they would have to leave their homes.

Janet had managed, for most of the time, to banish her speculations about the Englishman, memories of his devastating kiss, the feel of his hands holding her tight. She had worked at the most exhausting tasks she could devise. It was too disturbing, she told herself, to recall those sensations, or to wonder if he was one of the predatory foreigners who wanted to drive them off the land they'd lived on for centuries.

She'd heard of these men, and Iain

had encountered them, but she hadn't expected to meet them. Walking along this path, however, did not occupy her thoughts sufficiently, and they returned to Mr Fenton, and once more she felt his lips on hers.

Then Janet's thoughts were dragged back to the present. From the few words she caught, the children seemed to be urging Hamish, a big lad who ought to have been working in the fields, not larking about, to commit some mischief. She had almost come up to the children when Hamish suddenly stood up, drew back his arm, and threw something towards the track. There was a startled whinny, a muffled curse, and then a bright chestnut streak as a horse galloped wildly past the end of the path.

Janet knew that colour, and she ran the last few steps to the corner. The man, her Englishman, was picking himself up from the stony ground and glaring round him. Blood was pouring from a gash above his right eye.

'Who threw that stone?' he demanded, and heedless of his wound, strode towards the bushes where Hamish and his cronies were concealed.

Janet set down her pails hastily, and made for the bushes herself, calling angrily to Hamish. The boys had melted away. She could hear a few frightened giggles, but these children knew every tree, every hiding place, and if they wanted to vanish, they would.

Angrily, she swung round and almost collided with the Englishman. She would have fallen had he not clasped her arm, and as it was she was trembling with anger, and with the shock of seeing him again so suddenly. All too vividly, the memory of their first encounter, the feel of his lips on hers, flowed back into her mind.

'Where did they go?' he demanded. 'The little devils threw a stone and startled my horse. Is this how you bring up children, to attack harmless travellers?'

She took a deep breath to steady herself.

'I know who it was, I saw him, and you'll not catch them now, Mr Fenton. But I'll see they're punished. You're bleeding. Did the stone hit you? Let me see how badly you're hurt.'

He shrugged away from her hand.

'Don't fuss, woman. The stone hit my horse on his nose. I hit your cursed stony ground, but I'll not die from a mere cut. I must catch my horse, make sure he's not hurt.'

'It's all right, someone's caught him, look.'

Impatiently, he brushed the blood from his eyes.

One of the crofters, a small, bent old man, was leading the horse back along the track, talking gently to it as it sidled nervously, eyes wide with fear, its neck flecked with foam.

'Ye need to keep a firmer grip,' the old man said sternly as he handed the reins to Mr Fenton, with a barely-concealed sneer. 'If ye're no' accustomed to riding, ye need to take greater care.'

The Englishman stiffened, and Janet stifled a grin at the outraged expression on his face. No doubt he considered himself an excellent rider, but in his elegant clothes he would seem like a drawing-room dandy to a man like Dougal. He opened his mouth to protest, but some of the blood trickling down his face ran into his mouth and impatiently he spat it out. He turned away and examined the horse, but Janet could see no cuts. The animal had fared better than its master.

'Come and let me tend the wound,' she said before he could speak. 'Thank you, Dougal. It was that dratted Hamish. He chucked a big stone and hit the horse. No wonder Mr Fenton was unseated.'

'I was just dismounting,' Mr Fenton explained through gritted teeth. 'But I thank you.'

He fumbled in his purse for a coin,

but Dougal, with a contemptuous sniff, turned away.

'Keep your tainted English money,' he growled. 'We don't want it.'

'Come, let me see how bad it is before you lose more blood,' Janet urged, and turned to retrieve her pails.

Without waiting for him, she strode across to the cottage, thumped the pails down outside the door, and pointed to the bench set against the wall.

'Sit there while I get some rags and a salve.'

She glanced over her shoulder as she entered the cottage, and saw him tethering the horse to the ring set in the wall of the byre. With a hasty word of explanation to her grandmother, she collected what she wanted, poured a bowl of clean water from the pitcher she'd filled earlier at the well, and went back outside.

The cut was not deep, and had almost stopped bleeding. He had wiped away the blood with a handkerchief, and he held out a hand to ward her off as she approached. He'd brushed his hair to one side and she could see a white scar several inches long just on the hairline.

'I don't need your attentions, Janet Mackay. Not unless you are willing to talk to me as well.'

'Talk to you? Why? About what?'

She set down the bowl on the bench beside him, dipped in a cloth, and moved towards him. He grasped her hand and held it firmly away from his face. She trembled at his touch, the firm, smooth fingers which had so much strength in them, and instantly berated herself. She thought she'd managed to control her nervousness at these strange feelings, to thrust the memory of his kiss far down into her mind for most of the time, but this slight contact brought all the sensations flooding back.

'I want to know what's happening,' he went on, calm and apparently unaware of the effect he was having on her, 'but the crofters are too suspicious of me.'

'We don't like Englishmen,' she replied quietly. 'Now, for goodness' sake let me clean this cut and apply a salve to help it heal.'

He released her hand, and she forced herself to control the trembling which attacked her because of his nearness, and her recollection of his kisses. She wiped away the blood, patted his forehead dry, and dabbed on the ointment.

'That should heal in a day or so, and I doubt you'll be scarred, not like the other. Where did you get that?'

'Salamanca,' he said briefly.

'You're a soldier?' she asked, a note of incredulity in her voice.

He looked too smooth, too well groomed, to be a soldier, and then she noticed his broad shoulders, not obvious under the well-cut coat, and the strong muscles of his legs, and recalled the strength in his arms when he'd held her close.

'Why are you here in Scotland?' she added. 'Have you come to persecute us?

29

Has our countess's husband called in the military to drive poor people off his land?'

'So many questions,' he said mockingly. 'I was a soldier, but I sold out last year when my father died, as I had to take over running his estates. I've no intention of persecuting anyone. I knew your countess when I was a child in Paris, when she and her husband were at the embassy there. My father was posted there at the same time, but they would not remember me, and they do not know I am here. I came on my own account.'

He didn't say why, she noticed. He must be wealthy, if he had his own estates. He must wish to acquire land in Scotland, too, like so many Englishmen. She gathered up her things and turned to go into the cottage, to find her grandmother emerging, leaning heavily on a stick. She was looking at the visitor with interest.

Mr Fenton sprang up to help her, and Mary gave him a slight smile.

'Sit down, lad. Janet, fetch us some ale. It'll be better for our visitor than whisky, and I think he needs to rest awhile.'

Janet went inside but she could still hear the pair talking as she poured the ale.

'My thanks, Mistress Mackay. That is your name?'

'Yes, it is.'

'Everyone in the glen seems to bear that name.'

'Not all of us,' Mary said with a faint chuckle, 'but there are many cousins in Strathnaver village, like most clans. When we have to leave, though, we'll be scattered all over Scotland, and beyond.'

'So I understand. Can nothing be done? Won't your ministers help?'

'The lairds appoint the ministers, and most of them preach the will of God, and talk of our shortcomings, and rightful punishment.'

Janet, carrying two tankards of ale, paused in the doorway to look at them.

Her grandmother was unusually animated. Normally she regarded the few strangers who came to the glen with deep suspicion, but she was giving Mr Fenton the benefit of her sweetest smile.

'I'm beginning to understand the bonds which hold your clans together,' he said.

Mary nodded.

'Tell me, how did it happen that your horse unseated you? I heard you say you'd been a soldier.'

He grimaced.

'I was dismounting when some fool threw a stone which hit my horse on the nose. The poor brute started, and knocked me to the ground. I mean to find and punish the fool who could have blinded him.'

'It was Hamish,' Janet put in, 'but by now he'll be way up into the hills, and not back until nightfall. Here is your ale.'

'Thank you. Perhaps you can direct me to Hamish's father. It's not revenge for my loss of dignity,' he added, and Janet suppressed a smile. 'It was a foolish, dangerous thing to do, and he needs to be taught a lesson.'

'Leave it to his father,' Mary advised. 'He'll thrash him, but if you tried to, his father would be more likely to try and thrash you. The English are not welcome here.'

He raised his eyebrows slightly, eyebrows, Janet noticed, which were particularly well-shaped.

'So I have noticed. Yet you have an English overlord,' he said mildly. 'Or should I say laird? Is that the term?'

'Countess Elizabeth's our laird, not her English husband,' Mary told him. 'She's still the countess in Sutherland. We have no truck with English titles.'

'That hasn't stopped him interfering in our lives,' Janet added swiftly. 'He has wealth beyond counting, but he insists on raising the rents so much his tenants cannot pay, and then he turns them from their homes. No decent laird would behave so.'

'Others have done so,' Mary said beneath her breath, then she shook her head as if to clear it of such thoughts. 'Our guest doesn't want to hear about that,' she said more loudly, her voice harsh and unshed tears glistening in her eyes.

Janet turned abruptly and went to put away the salve and the bowl she'd used, but she could still hear their words, and she paused, listening, her lips twisted into a smile of disbelief.

'On the contrary, I am here to make a survey,' Mr Fenton was explaining. 'Perhaps I should not dignify it with such a high-sounding title, but my old commanding officer knew I had business in Glasgow, and he asked me to travel here first and judge, so far as a stranger, an Englishman, can, the extent of the unrest here.'

'Now Napoleon is defeated, sent to Elba, is the English army looking for new excitement here?' Janet demanded, returning to stand again in the doorway.

'Hush, child. There has been unrest

for two generations or more, since the best of our boys fell to English swords,' Mary said, so softly that Janet could scarcely hear.

'You mean Culloden?'

'Aye, but much worse now. The chiefs don't care for their people as they used to. They want higher rents so that they can flaunt themselves in finery, even as far away as London.'

'Not for the improvements?' he asked.

Janet could stand and listen to this in silence no more. She strode out of the cottage and stood, hands on hips, in front of him.

'Why do we need roads and bridges?' she demanded. 'It will only make it easier for foreigners to come here, to take our land, to patronise us for not living as they do.'

'Janet, my dear, our guest isn't responsible for that,' Mary intervened.

Janet shook her head impatiently. Mr Fenton was looking at her, a slight frown on his face.

'Surely it will help you, too?' he said

quietly. 'Better roads will mean the fishermen can take their catch to market, on carts, and faster, instead of so slowly on the backs of donkeys that the fish stinks by the time it reaches the buyers.'

'Fishermen, yes, but the crofters grow just enough for themselves. We have little to spare for selling, apart from the occasional sheep or cattle. The roads are to help those who want to breed hundreds of sheep on these hills, large flocks, driving us out to make room for them.'

'Is that what is happening here?'

'Yes, as in many parts of Sutherland,' Mary said, sighing.

Janet couldn't wait for her grandmother's quiet explanation.

'Some of the people went after the battle, for fear of reprisals. Now the lairds want us all to go, and the ministers preach at us to be obedient. At first it was by persuasion,' she said scornfully. 'Go to Canada, they said, there's good land aplenty there, and we'll pay your passage,' she mimicked. 'What they didn't say was that half the folk died on the journey, crammed into filthy ships, starved, and those who survived were so weak they couldn't lift a spade to till the soil!'

'Not all suffered so,' Mary reproved her. 'You know some are doing well, as Iain will.'

'Iain?' Mr Fenton asked.

Janet turned aside. She couldn't trust him. He was English, working for the military. It was because Iain had opposed the soldiers that her much-loved brother had been forced to flee, to leave his beloved Scotland and face the hazards of life in a strange, possibly dangerous new country.

Mary was explaining.

'My grandson,' she said quietly. 'He left Strathnaver last year to go to Nova Scotia. At least we know he's arrived safely, and soon, when I am gone, Janet will go to join him.'

Janet was thinking about the night Iain had struggled home, his arm broken where a soldier had clubbed him, deep cuts in one thigh from a sword, and his face heavily bruised. It had been good fortune which had enabled him to evade the soldiers looking for him, and they had hidden him in Mary's bed.

She smiled to recall how they had tricked the soldiers. Iain had been buried under the feather mattress so that he could scarce breathe, while Mary lay on top of the mattress beside him, feathers shaken to her side to hide the lump he made. Thanks to some artistic painting of blotches on her healthy skin, and several hot bricks wrapped in blankets and placed around her to cause sweating, she was so hot to touch that her claim of high fever and infection had been believed. Burning some foul-smelling plants on their small fire had made the atmosphere foetid, and the soldiers, after a cursory glance around, had retreated rapidly.

Afterwards, Iain, almost choking, had vowed he'd rather have been taken!

Janet, who had heard about conditions in some of the prisons, knew he didn't mean it.

Had the hold of the ship which had carried him to Nova Scotia been as bad, she wondered. He hadn't said much in his letter, just thankfulness to have arrived safely, and reassurances that his prospects of acquiring land farther west had been good.

Mr Fenton was now accepting Mary's offer of broth, simmering over the fire, and some of the bread Janet had made the previous day. Janet sighed. The tasks she had planned, the clearing and scouring of the byre now it was warm enough to turn the cow out during the day, would have to wait. More importantly, his presence was unsettling, a distraction she did not want.

She fetched a stool and placed it for a table in front of them, then filled two wooden bowls with the broth and took them outside. She took her own bowl and sat a few yards away on a fallen log, able to hear but not joining in their conversation.

She'd rarely seen Mary so animated since Iain had left. She almost preened, revelling in the attentions of a handsome young man, so that Janet felt ashamed for her, the first time she had ever allowed herself to criticise her grandmother. Then she felt angry with herself for that lack of generosity. Maybe Mary in some way associated Mr Fenton with Iain. He was, in his height and the colour of his hair, a little like Iain, and Mary knew she'd never again see her beloved grandson.

That was the fault of the English! Their countess Elizabeth's English husband had wanted to increase his already vast fortune. Some said he was the richest man in England, and the dowry he had received with his wife had consisted of two thirds of Sutherland. But it was poor land, and the rents were low because the people had barely enough to support themselves. They could not afford the higher rents he demanded. Suddenly some words of Mr Fenton's broke through her thoughts and she listened intently.

'The land cannot support all the people here, I'm told, so is not emigration the answer? Will they not be healthier, with better prospects, in a place like Canada, where the land is rich and fertile?'

'But this is our home!' Janet interrupted. 'We manage, and we're happy here. Your marquess cared nought for that. He threw off the poor people who couldn't afford to pay his increased rents, drove them out so that his English friends could fill the land with sheep!'

'Not my marquess, even though my estates in England are near his. I heard he offered them other land, by the coast,' Mr Fenton said.

'Yes, even more barren and desolate then here. They couldn't grow crops, they had neither the boats nor the skills to fish, and if they had, there was nowhere to sell the fish.'

'Until the new roads are built to take it to market.'

She glared at him.

'You're a soldier. Would you like to be told you can no longer be what you must choose, but must live in a ramshackle hut and earn your bread being a crossing sweeper, or a cobbler?'

'I lived in a few ramshackle huts in Portugal and Spain,' he said with a faint smile. 'But I do understand what you mean,' he added swiftly, holding up his hand to stem her furious reply. 'It is not the same, perhaps, but I would far rather be a soldier than have to manage estates which I had always assumed would go to my older brother.'

'He died?' Mary asked sympathetically.

'A hunting accident just a few weeks before my father died. I think that hastened my father's death. He had been about to marry, too. Sophia's estates are next to our land. It would have been a sensible match. But those are my worries, Mistress Mackay. I must thank you for your help and hospitality, and be on my way.'

'I hope to see you again, soon,' Mary said, and Janet glanced at her grandmother, wondering at the odd, almost pleading note in her voice.

'Of course. Farewell, Janet Mackay. We will meet again soon. I mean to stay in the district for a week or so longer.'

3

Mary was unusually quiet the following day, and Janet wondered if the visit of Mr Fenton had tired her. He had only remained an hour or so, but Mary had been unusually animated both during his visit and for the rest of the day.

She had spent the time sorting through her most valuable possessions, papers and a few trinkets her husband had given her, his pitifully few letters, and a necklace of cairngorms which had been his wedding present to her. There were also letters from her son and Janet herself, for she had written often as soon as she had been able to pen her letters.

She was awake early, however, looking cheerful and alert, and Janet breathed a sigh of relief. When they had to move, within weeks, her grandmother would need all her strength and courage.

'Janet, my love, I want you to take something to Mistress Ogilvie this morning. It's a reminder of the herbs I use for my salves. She asked me to write them down for her.'

Janet suppressed a sigh. It was a fine, sunny morning, and a strong, westerly breeze stirred the new leaves on the trees. She had planned to wash as many of their clothes as she could, ready to pack them before they had to move. Mistress Ogilvie lived a good four miles away, and even if she rode their small, sturdy pony, by the time she returned it would be too late to hope that the clothes could be washed and dried outside.

She would do as her grandmother wished, however. She fetched the pony from where he grazed in a nearby pasture, and slipped on the bridle. Kilting up her petticoats she scrambled on to his broad back, which was covered only by a rough blanket. Unlike the fine ladies in Edinburgh, and herself when she had lived there in luxury, she rode astride and without a saddle.

Mistress Ogilvie greeted her with tears in her eyes.

'Och, Janet, fancy Mary remembering this. It was just an idle fancy of mine, and I thought I'd never see you again once we'd driven away. But I won't see Mary. How is she? How does she bear the thought of leaving? I sometimes think it's all a terrible dream, and I don't know how I'm going to manage.'

'You have three sons to help you, as well as your man,' Janet said bracingly. 'You're going south, to Oban, I think?'

'Yes, they say there's work there.'

'When you're settled, write to us. Look, I've written down our location, in Thurso. At least my grandmother has somewhere to go.'

'And then you'll be after Iain, I suppose.'

Janet shook her head and blinked hard. She was so torn, wanting to join her brother, yet dreading what must come first.

'Not while she lives. I couldn't leave her, even with her own family.'

'Poor Mary! But, Janet, if you change your mind, you know my Duncan would be only too pleased to wed you.'

Janet nodded. Duncan Ogilvie had made it clear he admired her, but unlike Murdo Mackay he hadn't assumed she liked him, or tried to kiss her. She suppressed a shiver. Duncan was a good-looking man, a few years older than she was, quiet and dependable, but she could no more imagine being his wife than she could accept Murdo's courtship.

Mistress Ogilvie wanted to talk, to ask Janet's opinion on the best way to pack the family possessions, how to arrange them in the cart, and whether to kill the sheep before they left, and risk the meat going bad before they could sell it, or hope to drive their animals along with them.

'It's different with the cows,' she said fretfully. 'They can be tied to the cart, but we can hardly tether a dozen sheep trailing behind us.'

'The men and your dog will manage,' Janet tried to reassure her, and eventually she was able to say her farewells, promised to write, and set off back home.

Mary was sitting on the bench, half asleep in the sunshine, but she sat up, immediately alert, when Janet slipped from the pony's back. Janet eyed her carefully. She was flushed, and looked excited.

'I've sold my spinning-wheel,' she announced. 'That will be one less thing to bother with, and my hands can't spin any longer, and you won't want to when we leave here.'

That explained the excitement, the rosy cheeks, Janet thought with relief.

She had never been very adept at spinning, like the girls who had been taught from babyhood how to twist the strands of wool together. She had tried, but her thread had been lumpy and uneven, fit for nothing but the roughest blankets, Mary had said disparagingly.

Janet had thankfully turned her energies to things she could do more efficiently, and enjoyed doing.

It was later in the day, when she was spreading some of the clothes she had belatedly washed out on the bushes behind the croft, that she discovered another cause for Mary's satisfied look.

'Who's your grandmother's swain?' Katherine, who lived in the next cottage, asked.

Janet turned to look at her.

'What do you mean?'

'That handsome Englishman, who was here two days since, was here again today. Talking hard, they were, for an hour or more.'

She chuckled, a little maliciously, for her own daughter had been the most courted in the glen until Janet arrived.

'And I don't think it was you he came to see, or he'd have gone back the same way to meet you. He went up over the hills.'

Back to England, I hope, Janet thought,

as she tried to divert Katherine's attention by asking where they meant to go when they had to leave their home. Then, as soon as they could get away she went back to confront her grandmother. Mary was offhand.

'Oh, I think he said he was going farther up the glen today, and when he saw me sitting outside he stopped to thank us for our help, and show me that his cut was healing well.'

'Why didn't you tell me he'd been?'

'Are you interested in him?' Mary countered, and Janet shook her head hastily.

'Of course not, but we don't see many strangers, and you'd normally talk about any who come. I find it odd he should seek us out again. He must have more important things to do if he really is making a survey of feelings here.'

'He thinks there'll be trouble,' Mary said, and her voice quavered slightly.

'Trouble? You mean some of the men might try to resist?'

'Perhaps. There's some wild talk.'

'They'd be fools to do more than talk. Even that could be dangerous for them. The factors have the power to evict us, unjust though it is. If the men try to fight they'll be hurt, or put into prison, as Iain discovered.'

No more was said, but Janet lay in bed that night and tried to sort out her vague unease. She tried to put what she knew in some kind of order. Mary had sent her on a very trivial errand which had kept her away for hours and Mistress Ogilvie had not been expecting the list of herbs. Alastair Fenton, when he'd departed, had promised to visit again. Was Mary up to something? Had they arranged a precise time for him to come, while she had been out of hearing? And if so, why?

Then she remembered how Mary had been sorting through her precious few treasures. She rarely looked at them, explaining how recalling happier days was painful, and best avoided, though she could not bear to throw anything away. Had she, perhaps, asked him to perform some small kindness, perhaps deliver a message? But if so, what could it have been? Mary had lived all her life in Strathnaver, her only other close relative being her sister in Thurso. Her grandfather's brothers and sisters were dead, and their children had moved away long since, and were never heard from.

If Mary didn't want to say anything, it was none of Janet's business, she decided. Besides, the less she thought of the disturbing Mr Fenton, the better. He had reminded her of Edinburgh, the life she had lived before her parents died. Suppressed longings for a greater variety of activity and friendships had been awoken. She'd been content here with Mary, but she could not imagine living all her life here, cut off from the rest of the world.

Eventually she slept, to wake with a start as she heard a commotion outside the cottage. Men were shouting, women screaming, and children crying, and below all this noise was the sound of horses, several of them, moving about restlessly. Throwing a shawl over her nightshift, Janet went to the door and looked out. It was daylight, just, and a soft mist hid the trees and hills, isolating the small group of cottages and unexpected visitors.

At least half a dozen men were sitting on big, powerful horses, facing a crowd of angry crofters. Against the grey nothingness they looked huge and menacing. Janet shivered.

'Two days, and that's generous,' one of the horsemen said, glaring round at them.

'We were promised longer,' Katherine protested. 'Our rent's been paid. Ye've no right to turn us out before it's due next.'

Before the horseman could reply, a stone hit the horse's neck, and the animal reared in fright, scattering the others. More stones, less skilfully directed, fell amongst them. Janet saw Hamish and a few of his friends skulking behind Katherine's cottage. The horses were ridden out of range and set off farther up the glen.

'By nightfall tomorrow,' the riders called, their voices growing fainter as they disappeared round a bend in the track, lost in the swirling mist.

'We have to pack and go by tomorrow? Is that what they mean?' Janet asked, and Katherine nodded.

'You're getting lazy, asleep at this hour,' Katherine replied. 'Best start at once. There's a deal of work. They threatened to burn the houses whether we're out of them or not.'

Mary was sitting up in her bed, trying to struggle out. She was always stiff in the mornings, and needed help until her limbs became easier to move.

'I heard, lass,' she said, and sighed. 'So it's come, and earlier than we expected. You were restless last night.'

'So I slept late,' Janet said ruefully. 'I'll make your porridge, then I must begin loading the cart. It seems we have little time.'

Two days of frenzied activity followed. Mary, unable to do much to help, fretted as she watched Janet struggling to load heavy bundles and the smaller pieces of furniture on the cart.

'We can leave that chair. I don't want it,' she said on one occasion.

'It's the only one where you can sit in comfort, and grandfather made it,' Janet replied, stubbornly trying to lift the heavy chair on to an already overloaded cart.

She managed, but was bone-weary that night, and had to force herself to rise the following morning and deal with the mattress and other things they would need. The big bed was too cumbersome, and they knew it would be impossible to move it. Last of all, Janet lashed the box containing Mary's treasures and her own hoard of gold, her fare to Canada, to the back of the cart, and tethered the cow, lowing in bewilderment, to the tailgate.

Several of the crofters had constructed a makeshift camp on the slopes of the hill, where they planned to spend the night. The carts had been pulled into a defensive ring, and mattresses unloaded from them and spread on the ground.

'We dare not try to sleep in the houses,' they'd told Janet. 'Come and stay together, then we can move off at first light, and have the whole of tomorrow for travel.'

Mary sank down with relief. Even walking such a short distance up the hillside had taxed her strength. She and Janet knew she'd have to ride on the cart all the way to Thurso.

As Janet was spreading their blankets over her, there was a commotion from the north, the sounds of several horses galloping towards them. The men picked up what weapons they could find, mostly staves and billhooks, and moved to the edge of the circle. There was a shout from the riders, and one of the men laughed in relief.

'It's Mackay lads,' he shouted. 'That's my cousin, Jimmie.'

There were four of them, their clothes torn and their horses' sides flecked with foam. They rode up to the circle and flung themselves out of the saddles.

'What's to do, lads? Where's the fire?'

'Ye may laugh!' one of them replied angrily. 'There are fires all along the Strathnaver river and loch. They've no mercy. They're devils!'

'We were turned out without the chance to save any of our goods,' another said, and Janet recognised Murdo's voice. 'They set fire to the crofts. We had nought but what we wore, and couldn't go back for a thing!'

'Lucky to get away alive,' another said. 'Bruce here has a bullet graze in his leg.'

The women surrounded them anxiously, wanting all the gruesome details, but Janet turned away. What good would it be to dwell on these atrocities? She spread every blanket they had over her grandmother, and crawled in beside her. She could feel the old woman shaking with sobs and tears she had suppressed all day. Gently she cradled Mary to her, and eventually she fell asleep. Janet, however, remained wakeful, and after a while she heard shouts in the distance, followed by galloping hooves.

Cautiously she sat up. It was still not fully dark, but in the distance she could see flames lighting up the sky. Incredulous, she watched as new fires erupted all along the track. Others were watching, too. Janet rose and went to stand with them outside the ring of carts.

'They're nearer. They're firing our homes, too,' one woman wailed.

It was true. One by one, the crofts were being set alight, and soon the stone walls could be seen, eerily lit in silhouette against the flames. The roofs collapsed quickly, sending up showers of sparks, and the peat stacks caught fire and added to the noise and confusion.

Unable to stand the sight, a few of

the men seized what weapons they could and began to run down the hill.

'Come on lads, there's only half a dozen of the devils. We can stop them.'

'What's the use? We have to go anyway,' one of the woman wailed.

'And what good would it do if the devils were all killed, I don't know,' one of the women grumbled. 'They'd just send more, and punish us as well.'

Janet agreed silently, though she understood the impotent fury which demanded action.

Down in the township, a battle was raging, and in the faint light Janet saw the crofters fighting hand to hand with other men, attempting to drive them down towards the waters of the loch. The intruders fought back, and then, above the crackling of the fire and the murmurings of the watching crofters, a shot rang out. It was swiftly followed by several others, and a few of the men who had rushed so impetuously down the hill came scurrying back.

'They've shot young John,' one gasped.

'He had a gun, and he fired first.'

'No matter, he's sore wounded. Murdo, too.'

The rest of the would-be attackers came straggling back, carrying with them the shot man, pursued by half a dozen men with guns.

'If you try to interfere again it'll be the worse for you,' their leader snarled. 'I'm setting a guard down in the township for the night, and if you're not gone from Mr Sellar's land by sunrise your goods will be fired, too, and anyone remaining will be arrested and charged with obstructing the law.'

Murdo, supported by one of his friends from farther up the glen, came staggering up the hill and collapsed near to where Janet sat.

'Where did they hit you?' she asked, already busy unpacking her medicines.

'My leg,' he gasped. 'It's not bad, just a flesh wound, but it's bleeding and I have to stop that. I must hide. They know me, and they'll be after me, but if I bleed all over the place they'll be able to follow!'

'Stop talking. I'll bandage it for you,' Janet said, and Murdo quietened and allowed her to cleanse the wound on his calf as well as she could, and bandage it tightly.

'Why not stay with us?' she asked as he stood up, wincing.

'I daren't, I say. I think I killed one of their men earlier, and they'll know me. I'll be a danger to all of you. Help me mount the horse, and I'll hide in the woods.'

She gave him a napkin with some bread wrapped in it, and supported him as he limped to where someone else had tethered his horse. Groaning with the effort, he clambered into the saddle, and with a muttered word of thanks rode off as quietly as he could towards the path going south.

There was no more sleep for anyone. John was beyond help. The wound in his chest bled copiously, and within a very short time he breathed his last. His mother and sisters, stunned at the suddenness of the tragedy, wept over his body as others tried to comfort them.

Mary, to Janet's alarm, began gasping for breath and shivering, long before dawn. Then, hot and feverish, she began calling for Jamie. None of the women could calm her. None of the remedies they had helped, and all Janet could do was wipe away the perspiration and hold her grandmother's hand in hers.

The others began preparations for departure. None of them wanted to eat. They just loaded the mattresses on the carts and prepared to set off.

'We'll lift Mary up on top of the rest of your goods,' they said. 'You can't stay here alone.'

'She's too ill to move,' Janet protested.

'You daren't stay here alone,' Katherine insisted. 'Those brutes down there, well, you know what they'd do if they found you helpless.'

Janet knew there was no help for it, but when she saw her grandmother, strapped on to the cart for fear that in her delirious tossings she would fall to the ground, she felt like weeping with frustration and anguish. As the procession set off along the track, Mary grew worse, and the women shook their heads. They all knew the end was near.

A mile or so from the camp, the track passed through a small wood bordering the river.

'Help me to get the mattress down. I'll be hidden here, and I can't bear to see her die like this,' Janet said. 'I'll stay hidden until — until — '

Silently they nodded. They found a small clearing and lifted Mary down gently. One of the women milked the cow, and another placed some eggs in a nest of soft grass.

'You've water nearby. Don't light a fire, though.'

It was a long, dreadful day after they left. Janet unhitched the pony and hobbled it where it could graze, tied the cow to a tree, and sat beside her grandmother who was sleeping in snatches, between her restless spells when she seemed to imagine she was a girl again. Occasionally, she would take a sip of the milk, into which Janet had mixed one of the eggs, but most of the time she pushed the mug away.

As the sun began to sink lower, the air in the clearing grew cold, and Janet huddled into more clothes she unpacked from the bundles. More, and all the blankets they had, were piled on top of Mary, but she still shivered despite her hot, dry skin. Then, as Janet was despairingly contemplating the long night ahead, Mary opened her eyes and smiled.

'I'm sorry, lass,' she whispered. 'I'll be gone soon. Send word to Thurso, and get you to Glasgow and Canada. I'm sorry to leave you, but Jamie's waiting, and it's been such a long lifetime without him. Give Iain my dearest love, and God bless you.'

Mary then sank into a deep sleep,

and Janet held her grandmother's hands, tears streaming down her face. The moon rose and shed its ghostly, silver light into the clearing. After a while Janet felt her grandmother shudder, and there was just enough light to see her open her eyes for the last time, give a faint, sweet smile, and stop breathing.

Janet had managed to restrain her tears all day, but now she collapsed in despair, weeping convulsively as she clutched her grandmother's hand to her breast. Mary had been old, life for her had not been easy these past few years, full of pain, but it was a cruel way to die, driven from her home, out in the open like an animal.

Cradling the lifeless body to her, Janet eventually fell into a restless sleep herself. Her last thoughts had been a prayer that she could die, too, and accompany Mary wherever she was going.

4

For a few seconds when Janet woke, she could not think how they came to be lying on Mary's mattress under a canopy of leaves. She was cold, shivering in the dawn breezes, and as she reached for the blankets, her hand touched Mary's. It was cold and stiff, and Janet started up with an anguished cry, remembering.

It was true. She relinquished hope when she looked at her grandmother's peaceful, pale face, and knew she had been dead for hours.

Janet blinked hard as she milked the cow, wasting the milk for she had no means of carrying it, then she sluggishly tried to plan what to do. Mary must be buried decently, but where could she find a minister, and how was she to carry Mary's body there? She shivered, and little though she wanted to eat, she knew she had to be strong so as to perform the last services she could for Mary.

She went down to the river and splashed cold water on her face. She'd have liked to bathe properly, to drive away the weariness and the traces of two nights sleeping in the open, but the water, fed by mountain streams, was bitterly cold, and she was afraid of becoming too numb to do what must be done.

As she walked back to the clearing, she was wondering whether it would be safe to go back past the loch towards Syre, or better to continue southwards.

The men who had driven them out were to the north, and would be unlikely to help her. Better to go south, despite not knowing what she might find there.

It could take two or three days to reach a sizeable township where there might be a minister, but the chances of being able to bury Mary decently would be greater. Janet was determined to honour the woman who had been everything to her for the past few years, as much as was within her power.

She had just come to her decision when she returned from the stream and arrived back in the clearing. A man, his back towards her, was bending over Mary's body, and Janet, terrified of what he might be doing, ran forward, crying out to him in fury.

'Leave her alone!'

'Hush, Janet, it's only me,' the man said, standing up and taking her by the shoulders.

'Murdo! Why are you here? How did you find us? And how is your leg? Has it stopped bleeding?'

'I'm all right. It's painful, but no more. Janet, they've fired all the houses! I went back, just to see, as soon as it was light, and they're all gone. And the crofters, they'd moved on. I thought you'd be with them.'

He tried to put his arm round her shoulders but she moved away to sit on a fallen log. He came and stood with one foot on the log, looking down at her with compassion in his eyes.

'I saw what had happened to your house. Burned to the ground, it was, the same as with us. I thought you'd moved with the others and I rode after you. The women told me that Mary was mortally sick, and where they had left you. I'm sorry.'

Janet nodded her thanks.

'She died last night. I still can't really believe it. I have to find a minister to bury her.'

'Aye. We'll go back to Syre, and ask where the minister is. Sellar's men will be able to tell us. Most of the ministers have been supporting the changes, preaching that we have to accept God's will.'

'So that they can save their own livings. No, Murdo, I'll not ask for help from any of them. I'll take her south, find someone there.'

'But, Janet, she'd wish to be buried in her own glen, among her kinsfolk,' Murdo pointed out.

Janet shook her head.

'The only one who mattered to her was Jamie, and his body was never found after Culloden,' she declared.

Rising from the log, she went to the cart and began to remove some of the bundles. She tipped the big chair from the top, and it fell crashing to the ground.

Murdo uttered an exclamation of protest.

'Janet, take care! It'll splinter, treated like that.'

She barely glanced at him as she threw more of the bundles to the ground.

'What does that matter? She has no more use for it,' Janet replied, her voice filled with despair.

'But others might,' he began. 'Janet, I know now's not the time to talk about the future . . .'

'I have to think of it,' she interrupted angrily.

It had all been too sudden, and combined with their eviction, she'd had no time to plan or even think beyond the next urgent step. It was fate and she was railing against the men who'd treated them so harshly, but Murdo's shoulders sagged as though she had vented her fury on him.

'Ye're not alone now,' he muttered.

'I'll take just what I'll need on the journey to Glasgow, until I can get a ship,' she said slowly.

She thought briefly back to the plans they had made a year or more ago, for the time she'd be free to leave Scotland. Now, once she had safely buried her grandmother, she could set off to rejoin her brother. A sudden small glimmer of excitement sprang into being deep within her. There was some sort of future, after all.

Murdo was picking up the bundles lying around them, and stood clutching them to him.

'Others might have a use for them. Be sensible, Janet. You could sell the chair, or we might use it when we've found a place of our own. Ye don't have to risk your life on those pesky ships.'

'A what?' Janet turned and stared at him. 'What do you mean, a place of our own? I'll be going to Canada now, to join Iain and I can't take any of this with me.'

He pushed back his hair, and a slow blush became visible above his beard.

'I meant, well, Janet, you know how I feel about you. I always hoped you'd wed me one day, and now you haven't to care for your grandmother, you're free.'

Janet sighed. She had been wrong to permit those kisses, when she first came to the glen, but she'd been young, lonely, sorry for him left alone when his parents died, for he had no brothers and his only sister had married and gone to Edinburgh.

And, she confessed to herself, she had been curious about what it would feel like to be in a man's arms. She'd tried to avoid Murdo the past year, and made sure they'd never be alone.

Suddenly she thought of the kiss the

Englishman, Alastair Fenton, had given her up on the hillside so recently. It had been so different, so much more exciting.

'No, Murdo, I never said I'd wed you. I'm going to join Iain,' she said eventually.

'The journey's dangerous, I tell you. So many die. Why not stay here? We'll get to Glasgow, I'll find work, and we can be happy. I love you, Janet. I have done for years.'

Janet shook her head slowly, and turned back to shifting the bundles about.

'No, Murdo. I'm sorry, but I don't love you, and I'll never wed where I can't love.'

'You're upset, it's natural, but you'll feel differently soon. I love you, I say, and that will be enough for now. You'll forget Mary, this dreadful time, and I'll make you love me.'

She knew he was not being intentionally insensitive, but she was feeling too raw to make allowances.

'I'll never forget my grandmother! How dare you even suggest it?' she exclaimed.

He shrugged.

'People do forget. Well, not exactly forget, but the pain gets less. I know. It did when my parents died, and that was only two years ago. Janet, stop throwing useful things off the cart. You'll need them.'

'She never forgot my grandfather,' Janet said softly, 'and the pain was as great yesterday as the day it happened. I'm making a place to lay her down. I don't need these things. You can have them, but I'm going to Canada.'

'You don't need that soft couch,' he said, taking her by the arm. 'Mary won't feel the lumps now.'

Janet shook him off.

'No, but I'll feel them for her. She'll have comfort for her last journey. Now, Murdo, I'd be grateful if you'd help me lift her up on to the cart. Gently, mind.'

Frowning, he did as she directed, then harnessed the pony and tied the cow's halter to the back of the cart. As Janet was about to set off back towards the track, he protested.

'You could put the bundles round Mary's body, and then balance the chair on top,' he suggested.

Janet turned on him in absolute fury. Would he never understand, never give up?

'I'm grateful for your help, Murdo, but she is my grandmother, they are my things, and I will decide what to do. If you want to gather them up and sell them, you're welcome.'

He glanced at her, then looked back at the discarded chair and various bundles and then, limping, went to fetch the horse he'd tethered to a low branch.

'I think you're daft, but it's as you wish.'

'Yes.'

In silence, they went back to the main track, Murdo riding ahead, Janet driving the cart. For a mile or more he stayed ahead, even though the track here was wide enough for him to ride alongside, and Janet wondered if she had offended him too much, but she could never marry him, and surely he ought to have known that.

She wondered what he had done with his own possessions. All he carried were saddlebags and a roll of blanket tied to the saddle. Had he not had time to save more, or had he decided that trying to take more would be pointless?

She would not have brought so much if it hadn't been for Mary. When her grandmother was safely buried she would abandon all but her clothes and her few precious possessions, sell them if she could, sell the cow and the cart and ride the pony the rest of the way.

They forded a small stream and Murdo, glancing back to check that the cart didn't get stuck in the mud, waited for her and gave her an apologetic grin.

'Sorry,' he muttered gruffly. 'I shouldn't have bothered you now.'

Janet forgave him.

'I was upset,' she apologised in her

turn. 'Let's forget about it.'

They travelled on in silence, but it was a comfortable, companionable silence, broken only by an occasional comment. There were other people going the same way. They all had tales to relate of horrific treatment by Sellar's men.

'They tried to burn the house before the old man was out, and him bedridden,' one woman told them indignantly. 'It was a miracle his neighbours were able to get to him through all the smoke.'

Janet and Murdo listened in horror.

They had paused beside a large group to eat the bread and meat Murdo had in one of his pockets.

'Set fire to the heather and the peat, and what was left of our barns,' another woman said, swallowing her sobs.

'They forced young Flora out to sleep in the open, and she with child. She miscarried during the night, poor lass, and none of us could save her. She bled to death.'

Murdo looked at Janet.

'We can go faster on our own,' he suggested. 'They have so much to carry, their carts are overloaded, and their animals are slow. The old people have to walk, and they can only do a few miles each day. We could get to Glasgow weeks before they do.'

Janet nodded.

'But wouldn't it be more protection to travel in a group?'

'What can we do? If the soldiers follow, they'll be helpless. Just the two of us, we might have more chance of hiding.'

He was right, but Janet was reluctant to go with him. He could read more into that than she was prepared to allow.

Before she could answer, a horseman, galloping hard, was seen coming towards them.

'It's them!' one woman screamed, and began to run away from the track and into the shelter of some trees.

Her husband, in a few short steps,

caught up with her and forced her to stop.

'Don't be daft, woman! It's only one man. He can't hurt us,' her husband said gruffly.

Janet was staring at the man, recognising the bright chestnut of the horse he rode before she could distinguish his features. Her heart was beating erratically, and she could feel her cheeks grow warm.

'It's that devil of an Englishman!' Murdo exclaimed. 'What does he want here?'

Alastair swung out of the saddle, ignored the men who had jumped up, weapons in hand to defend the small group, glanced briefly across at the cart where Mary's body lay, and then he strode across to glare down at Janet where she sat motionless.

'Where the devil have you been? How did I miss you? I rode as far as I thought you could have travelled, and I was afraid the men had taken you prisoner.'

Janet raised her eyebrows in astonishment.

'Why on earth should they do that?'

'Your brother's a fugitive, a wanted man, and they might think to persuade you to tell them where he is.'

'He's in Canada and they must know that! It's no secret. But what has it to do with you?'

He sighed, gave her a reluctant grin, and then sank down on the turf beside her.

'Mary said you'd be difficult. She's asleep, I see. The upheaval must have been hard for her,' he said, glancing round at the small group of travellers avidly listening to him.

'She's dead,' Janet whispered, her voice wavering.

All day she'd restrained the tears, but it was hard, and she was bone-weary.

'I need to find a minister to bury her.'

'Dead? You poor child,' he said, and flung his arms around her shoulders to draw her close to him. 'Don't worry, I'll see to everything now. I'll make all the necessary arrangements for you.'

Janet wanted to pull away. She could hear the scandalised exclamations of some of the women, but his arms were so comforting, his chest so broad, and his human warmth so reassuring after the horrors of the past few days that she relaxed, sinking against him, heedless for the moment of anything but the comfort he represented.

It was Murdo's shocked rebuke that brought her back to reality and made her push herself away from Mr Fenton.

'There's no cause for such behaviour, Janet,' Murdo said, clearly furious. 'As for you, Englishman, I'll thank you to keep out of our affairs. Your countrymen have brought enough harm to Scotland. I can take care of Janet and her poor grandmother. They are kin.'

'I'm sure you could do so, but I promised Mistress Mackay I'd take care of Mistress Janet if anything happened to her. She knew the end was near, though I doubt she expected it to come like this.'

Murdo protested, and was supported by most of the other men in the group, who resented this stranger, this Englishman, coming in and taking charge.

Alastair listened patiently to their protests, until, bewildered by his calm refusal to argue, they fell silent.

Janet thought she now knew why her grandmother had sent her on that trivial errand to deliver the medicinals so that she could talk to Alastair alone.

She was confused, even angry that her grandmother should have trusted a stranger, yet in an odd sort of way he inspired trust, and she had no right to be angry with poor Mary, who had probably thought she was reluctant to accept Murdo's help, knowing he would take it as encouragement when she had no desire to do as he wished, and marry him.

The matter was decided when Alastair smiled gently round at the group and held out his arm to Janet.

'We'd best be on our way,' he said with such tenderness. 'There's an inn of sorts where we can rest tonight, and a minister no more than ten miles farther on. Can you drive the cart, or shall I hitch my horse alongside the cow?'

★　★　★

The afternoon passed in a haze. It was fortunate the pony was docile, for Janet half-slept as she drove along. They could not travel fast, but they soon left the rest of the group behind, muttering amongst themselves. Only Murdo, his voice often raised in angry protest, followed to go with them.

As they reached the inn, the inn-keeper appeared from the door, looking flustered.

'I'm sorry, I have no room,' he said, holding his arms wide as if to bar their way.

Alastair swung from the saddle and taking his arm, led the man a short distance away. Murdo drew close to the cart and leaned down to speak softly to Janet.

'Ye can't just let him take over, Janet,' he said urgently. 'Ye don't know what he wants but I doubt it's honourable, not like me. I want to wed you and look after you.'

'Murdo, it's no good,' Janet said. 'He's being kind, that's all I care about, and he probably knows more than either you or I do about all this. You've hardly left the glen all your life.'

Janet watched Alastair talking to the innkeeper, who nodded, and after a few moments turned and smiled at her.

'I'm sorry for your trouble, lass. I've only a small room, my son's, but he's away right now, and you're more than welcome to it. Your man here has agreed to sleep in the hayloft, while your poor grandmother lies at rest in the barn. He,' he added, nodding towards where Murdo stood, 'can sleep in the hay as well.'

Janet, thankful to be relieved of responsibility, followed the innkeeper inside and was handed over to his wife, who murmured in sympathy and insisted on bringing a bowl of broth and some bread and cheese up to the room.

'You'll be better alone,' she said, nodding to herself. 'We've a whole group here tonight, a rough-looking lot, some of them, and angry at being turned off their crofts. Best you keep out of their way.'

The room was tiny, but Janet was thankful to be alone, to give way at last to her grief. She was almost too tired to eat, but the broth was warm and comforting, and she forced herself to swallow some of the bread and cheese. The next day would be difficult, saying a final farewell to her grandmother.

On the following day, Mary was laid to rest in a small churchyard, and after a last, lingering look at the hastily filled-in grave, Janet squared her shoulders and turned to face the future — Glasgow and then Canada.

5

When the track was wide enough, Murdo brought his horse alongside the cart, sometimes jostling to get in front of Alastair. He, however, seemed content to ride behind them, to Janet's regret. She was still weary, desolate at the final parting with her grandmother, and wanted peace to come to terms with her loss. Murdo's repeated urgings that she marry him eventually made her turn on him in fury.

'Murdo, leave me alone! I don't want to marry you, and the more you pester me now the less likely I ever will.'

Murdo looked at her, a hurt expression in his eyes.

'I only want to protect you,' he muttered, 'but I suppose you think I've nothing to give you, no money for fine clothes, like wealthy Englishmen can provide.'

'I'm going to Canada! I don't want fine clothes!'

'You're just bemused with that smooth Englishman flinging round his money and his orders.'

'Would the innkeeper have let us stay if he hadn't been there?'

'He'd have listened to me.'

'Unlikely! And would the minister have agreed to bury Grandmother? I don't think so, and I'm grateful to him, but nothing more.'

'He'll ask for payment, you see! Englishmen are all the same. They take what they want by force, or soft words and promises that mean nought.'

'You don't know him. He's not your rival, Murdo, and I mean nought to him. He's merely being kind because Mary asked him to help. She knew it was near the end.'

She spoke vehemently, and Murdo had to drop back as the track narrowed, passing through a wooded area, but Janet wondered whether she had not protested too strongly. Alastair had kissed her, after all. Was he, as Murdo suggested, likely to demand payment? Was he attracted to her more than for just casual dalliance? Would he expect her compliance? Was that why he had been so helpful?

He wasn't like that, she was sure. He would not exact a reward such as Murdo, jealous and possessive, predicted. She thought back to that first, devastating kiss, and felt a slight tremor deep within her. No man had ever kissed her like that, and when he had held her in his arms for comfort, he had felt warm and strong and reliable.

She sat up straighter. He meant nothing to her, just someone who had snatched a kiss when the chance arose, which ought to make her wary, but didn't, and his kindness since had had a brotherly feel about it. It was how Iain would have behaved, no more. Soon she would be on her way to rejoin Iain. It had been her plan, and she could now think of the details. How soon might she expect to find a passage from

Glasgow? The ships taking the emigrants on the long voyage to Nova Scotia left frequently, she'd heard. Luckily it was still early summer, so there was time to make the crossing before the winter gales stopped them.

Thoughts of what Canada was like, recollections from Iain's letter describing the harsh country near Halifax, occupied her until she was jolted back to the present by shouts coming from the densely-growing trees on either side of the narrow path. The pony reared in fright, and would have bolted had two men not leaped forward and hauled on the reins. Several others surrounded the cart, and one reached up, grabbed Janet round the waist, and dragged her to the ground.

She fought viciously, biting and kicking, and he swore loudly as her boots connected with his shins.

'Ye'll pay for that!' he growled, pulling her towards him and imprisoning both of her arms behind her back with one hand while with the other he tried to turn her face towards his. 'Ye're a beauty, a wildcat, but we'll tame ye.'

'You'll do no such thing.'

It was Alastair's voice and Janet sagged in relief, then took the opportunity of her captor's relaxing his grip to drag free. She glanced behind her to see Alastair, still mounted, pointing two pistols at the men. Murdo was tussling with one of them, both rolling on the ground, but the others, four or five, had drawn back from the cart and were regarding Alastair warily.

'Murdo!'

Alastair's brusque tone penetrated to the men on the ground, and they looked up. Murdo struggled to his feet, kicking the other as he did so.

'Shoot them,' he panted.

'Don't be a fool. Get some of the rope that ties the bundles, but don't get in between them and my line of fire. You can tie them up.'

Murdo began to protest that they should be killed, that it wasn't safe to leave them alive, but Janet nodded and moved towards the cart. Careful not to block Alastair's aim, she quickly found a spare hank of rope which had been used to secure the abandoned chair. She took it behind the men and began securing their hands behind their backs. Murdo hovered behind her, demanding to be allowed to take over, but she shook her head and curtly told him to keep away and stop distracting her. Having nothing with which to cut the rope, she simply hooked the men all together, until she had all the attackers imprisoned.

'Well done,' Alastair said, chuckling as he dismounted and put away his pistols. 'We'll tie them to a tree, and it will take them some time, I think, to find a way out of that tangle. Murdo, go and catch your horse. He won't have gone far.'

He led the imprisoned men, stumbling, spitting and cursing, farther into the wood until he found a tree to which he could lash the ends of the rope, well above their heads.

'That should keep them occupied for a while,' he murmured.

'I didn't know you carried pistols,' Janet said as they walked back to the cart.

'Fortunate that I do,' he replied easily. 'They were other poor dispossessed devils, I imagine. Soldiers would have been more organised. These men seemed rather desperate.'

'They will be able to get free, won't they?' Janet asked. 'They won't die there.'

'Of course not! If they can't find a way of undoing the ropes, they'll be heard by other travellers,' he said, laughing, and Janet grinned.

She, too, could hear the frantic shouts for help coming from behind them.

'We'd better rid ourselves of the cart and the cow as soon as possible, though,' Alastair said as he picked her up and lifted her back into the driving seat before she knew what was happening. 'It slows us down, and you won't need to keep more than the absolute essentials, for I'll look after you now.'

Murdo, who had been standing moodily beside the cart, holding his own horse's bridle, began to protest that the cart was useful, but Alastair cut him short.

'Let's move. It may not take them very long to free themselves, and they'll be thirsting for vengeance.'

There were no more chances for talk as they travelled on. Janet's thoughts were confused. What had he meant? What had Mary made him promise to do? Did he merely intend to escort her to a ship, or had there been something more sinister in his promise to look after her? Was Murdo right after all?

She hoped not. She had trusted Alastair, was coming to rely on him, and been grateful to him for his help, but she would not become his mistress, if that was his intention. And what else could he mean? Marriage, the only other interpretation, was out of the question even if she would agree, and she was going to Canada.

He was wealthy, owned English estates, and though he hadn't said it, surely there would be pressure on him to marry the heiress who had been promised to his late brother. What was her name? Sophia, she remembered, with estates adjacent to his. It would be an ideal match, as Janet knew. For the aristocracy and landowners, marriage was a calculated arrangement. Not for them the pairing from inclination and choice of the lower orders. Had her own parents lived, she would no doubt have been married off to a man who could enlarge her father's business.

Her musings were interrupted as they approached a large village. Alastair led them to the shade of a large oak, and Janet was soon busy sorting out the essentials she could carry on the pony while she rode. It was not a great deal — a few clothes, her letter from Iain, her own store of gold coins and Mary's few jewels in the small box where Mary had always kept her most precious possessions. The rest of it she was happy to sell, and soon Alastair, who had been to the nearby inn, returned with a couple of men who were interested in the cow and the cart.

They haggled, but Alastair haggled back, and soon a price was agreed, better than Janet had expected. The cow was led away, and the other man fetched a pony to hitch to the cart. Alastair handed Janet a bag full of coins. She was busy arranging the bundles she still had behind the rug which would serve as her saddle, and strapping the box between them.

'Thank you. I didn't expect to get such a good price,' she said to Alastair.

'Put it away safely.'

She opened the box, and blinked in astonishment, and then began to search frantically in the small, wooden box.

'No! It must be here!' she exclaimed.

'Janet? What is it?' Alastair queried.

'My money, the gold I had to pay my passage! It's gone!'

'Are you certain? Has it slipped

under something else?'

Janet shook her head.

'I've looked. There isn't much else, nothing big enough to hide it. Look for yourself.'

'Ye don't need it, I tell you,' Murdo said. 'I'll provide all we need.'

Janet ignored him. She was trying to think. Who had been near her box? When could it have been taken?

'Those men who attacked us, they didn't have a chance to open the box, did they?'

Alastair took hold of her hand and stroked it to still the trembling.

'Steady, now. Let's try and work it out. When did you last see the gold?'

Janet took a deep breath and tried to think calmly. She clung to Alastair's hand. His touch was comforting.

'Before we left the cottage, when I loaded it on to the cart.'

'So there have been times when the cart has been left, when anyone could have stolen it.'

Janet forced herself to think.

'Yes. The first night when we had to sleep on the hillside, when I helped Murdo away, after he'd been wounded. Then there was the night Mary died. I was alone, and in the morning I went to the river to wash. I left the cart. Did you see anyone around, Murdo, when you came, before I got back?'

He shook his head.

'I heard some rustling, but it could have been deer, or foxes. There was also the night Mr Fenton made us leave poor Mary's body in the barn.'

'Did you hear anything?' Janet asked.

Alastair shook his head.

'We were right above it in the hayloft. We'd have heard. Besides, the barn door was secured inside with an iron bar. That would have made enough noise to wake me. Murdo, did you hear anything that night?'

'No, but as I tell Janet, it doesn't matter. I'll look after her.'

'I'm going to Canada!' Janet said, exasperated, and then she realised that without the gold she could not pay her passage. 'But now I don't have the money.'

She thought hard.

'I might have enough if I took a ship to Ireland. The cost's less in their ships.'

'And from all I've heard they are leaky old tubs, riddled with vermin. Half of them never get there and on the others most of the passengers die!' Alastair said bluntly. 'You can't go on one of them. Besides, would you have enough to keep you until you could follow your brother to wherever he's gone? Canada is a huge place. It could take months before you found him.'

'Then I'll have to find a job in Glasgow,' she said. 'How long do you think it will take me to earn enough?'

Was Alastair trying to deter her? And if so, why? What did he want of her? Was Murdo right, that he would expect payment for the help he was giving them?

'You don't need to,' Murdo repeated. 'I'll find a job.'

Neither Janet nor Alastair paid him

any attention. At the same time Alastair spoke.

'We can't think about it now, Janet. Let's get on our way, and we can make plans when we've reached Glasgow.'

It took over a week, during which they slept in the open, rolled up in cloaks on beds of heather. They passed other groups of travellers, stopping to exchange news and talks of plans. Many were going to Canada, and Janet absorbed all she could of what they knew about the new country.

She was weary of riding by the time Alastair drew rein outside a large new house on the west of the city.

'We'll be able to stay here,' he said.

Janet looked dubious. Would they accept her, bedraggled as she was after so long a journey? It was a district where many new houses had been built by the wealthy merchants and lairds. It was late, after sunset, and Janet forgot her doubts as she thought longingly about whether she would be able to lie on a soft mattress this night.

'A cousin's house,' Alastair explained.

He plied the knocker and the door was opened promptly by a liveried manservant, who expressed no surprise to be confronted by three travel-stained riders. Murdo, who had been moody during the entire journey, drew back.

'I'll be away to find myself a bed,' he muttered. 'I doubt I'll be welcome here, in this fine house. Now I know where you are, Janet, I'll come and talk with you tomorrow.'

Alastair merely nodded, and turned to help Janet dismount. As she passed through into the wide hallway she turned and saw Murdo, suddenly looking forlorn, his shoulders drooping, riding away. Then her attention was taken up with greetings from Alastair's cousin, a woman a few years older than he was, and her husband, a wealthy merchant who owned, they told her later, several silk works.

Gordon and Margaret MacBeith seemed delighted to welcome their unexpected guests, and Margaret hustled Janet upstairs, calling to the maids to bring water, quickly.

'You'll like a bath, no doubt, and some supper in your room, in peace,' she suggested, and Janet smiled thankfully at her.

She did not feel like making polite conversation to strangers, and besides, her gowns were all crumpled, and not at all fine enough to wear in this luxurious house. For a moment she thought wistfully of the gowns she had possessed in her own home in Edinburgh, but thrust the thought aside.

She would never again have the need for silks and satins. Her working gowns, all she had kept, which had been her normal attire in Strathnaver, would serve while she worked to raise money for a more comfortable, safer passage, and no doubt in Canada she would need the same, for life there would be hard, too.

Several maids bustled about, lighting the fire in Janet's bedroom, filling the bath they set in front of it from steaming copper cans, warming thick, soft towels, and whisking away her clothes to wash and iron. She felt pampered, and sank down into the soft, scented water with a sigh of sheer bliss. It was the first time, she thought, that she had felt truly content since Mary had died.

Afterwards, a tray appeared, borne by a plump, motherly woman who announced with an English accent that she was Mistress MacBeith's personal maid, and if there was anything Mistress Mackay wanted of her, she would be very happy to oblige.

'You're to be left to sleep in the morning, but when you are ready to eat, ring the bell and a tray will be brought.'

Janet was soon asleep, and even the unaccustomed noises of a town did not disturb her. The sun was high in the sky when she awoke, to find the fire burning cheerfully, her freshly-laundered gowns hanging on hooks, and a bowl of hot water waiting for her on the washing stand.

She washed, revelling in the luxury of it, and rang the bell. A maid appeared almost at once, bearing a tray with porridge, thin slices of bread and butter, a dish of tea and one of chocolate.

'We didn't know which you'd prefer,' she said, bobbing a curtsey, 'so cook said to bring both. And is there anything else you'd like? Some cold beef, perhaps, or ham?'

'No, nothing, this is perfect,' Janet reassured her.

'Then I'll come back later to help you dress and show you to the mistress's room,' the girl said.

Janet nodded, but she had dressed herself in her best gown before the maid reappeared. She'd never have her own maid, though if her parents had not died she would soon have been provided with one, as she began to go about in Society. Seeing the little maid's anxiety at having been, as she thought, late, neglecting her duties, Janet tried to reassure her, and allowed her to brush out her long hair which, from having been washed the previous evening, was in a fly-away state and difficult to control. In the end, Janet secured it with a ribbon and tied it in a loose knot on top of her head.

When Jeannie, as the maid shyly told her she was called, was satisfied, she led Janet down a flight of wide stairs to the room she called the boudoir, where Margaret MacBeith was sitting at a small table teaching a little girl of about five to write, using a small slate.

She turned and rose to greet Janet.

'My, you look so much better. I hope you slept well.'

'Wonderfully,' Janet replied. 'I am so sorry I'm so late. It's rude of me.'

'Not at all. From what Alastair tells me you've had a difficult time, and you must have been exhausted. This is my daughter, Flora. Say good morning to our guest, Flora, then you must run away. Your lesson is over for the day.'

The child, dark, petite, and with an

enchanting smile, curtseyed and almost fell over. She giggled gleefully and went off skipping, holding Jeannie's hand.

'What a delightful child!' Janet said.

'She's the joy of our lives,' Margaret replied, and then looked solemn again. 'I was so sorry to hear about your grandmother. She must have been a remarkable lady. Alastair was most impressed with her. He tells me, too, that he promised her to look after you.'

'Which he has done,' Janet said hastily, 'but I must not trespass on your hospitality for too long. I need to find a position of some sort, to earn my passage to Canada. My brother is waiting there for me to join him.'

'He had to leave in a hurry, I believe,' Margaret said delicately.

Janet nodded.

'I'd have gone with him, but my grandmother needed me, too. He was being hunted by the English soldiers.'

'Yes. Alastair said something about it.'

Janet decided she could confide in Margaret.

'He was betrothed to a girl who lived in another glen. He went to visit her, but there was fighting when the people were being evicted. His girl was killed. Iain led the men against the factors and the soldiers, and someone, a man he'd known when we lived in Edinburgh, recognised him. They, the soldiers, came to Strathnaver in search of him then Iain was injured, but they knew who he was, and that he'd probably find his way back to us. They came to find him. He had to flee. It was the only way he could escape being put in prison, and probably hanged.'

'You poor child. Have you heard from him?'

'One letter, and he knows I will be following him. He has left word in Halifax of where I can find him, but I need to earn the money. What I had was stolen.'

'So Alastair said. But you don't need to face that dreadful journey, you know.

Alastair will look after you.'

Janet shook her head.

'I couldn't allow it. He's been so kind already. I can't ask more of him. And I must go to join Iain. We only have each other now.'

'We'll see. Now, are you ready to face the world? I have another guest staying.'

'This is the best dress I have and it's not fit for company,' Janet protested. 'I had only serviceable gowns for working in while I lived in the glen.'

'No matter. You still look charming, my dear. Come, we'll go to the drawing-room.'

She led the way swiftly and Janet had to follow. She shrugged. Why should she care how she looked? She would be gone from here as soon as she could obtain some position.

Margaret entered the drawing-room and Janet looked about her in appreciation. It was a large, well-proportioned room, hung with delicate silk wallcoverings in pale green, curtains of a deeper green at the windows, the same shade repeated in the pattern of the cream carpet. The elegant, light furniture which was fashionable, she knew, in London and Edinburgh, was arranged to enhance the space, and some delightful landscapes by someone Janet recognised as a master hung on the walls.

It was a moment before she realised Margaret was introducing her to a small, very pretty blonde girl a year or so older than herself, who reclined languidly on a claw-footed sofa.

'Sophia, may I present Janet Mackay? She has had the most incredible adventures escaping from persecution. Janet, this is Sophia Constantine, who was betrothed to Alastair's poor brother, and who lives next door to him in Staffordshire.'

6

Sophie smiled at Janet. She really was pretty, with her pink and white complexion and fair hair cut in what Janet thought must be the latest style, a mass of short, frond-like curls.

'You have been having an utterly abominable time, haven't you? Dear Alastair told us last night. Poor love, he was so upset that he hadn't been able to prevent the theft of your money. He wants to give you the same amount, and you must let him. He can well afford it,' she added hurriedly as Janet began to shake her head. 'I was sorry to hear about your grandmother.'

'Thank you, but I couldn't possibly accept any money from him. The theft was nothing to do with him,' Janet replied.

So this was the girl Alastair would probably marry? She was lovely, and it seemed as though she was good-natured, too.

Janet felt a sudden wave of fury towards Alastair, who had treated her with familiarity, hugging and kissing her, when he had this lovely girl waiting for him.

'Come and sit down and tell me all about what is happening. If you feel you can, that is,' Sophie added, patting the seat beside her.

Inwardly, Janet sighed. She wanted to forget, but she could hardly snub Sophia.

As she talked, as briefly and unemotionally as she could, she resolved that she had to leave this household as soon as possible. The difficulty was how. She would not, she suspected, be permitted to roam Glasgow on her own, seeking to become a chambermaid or obtain a similar position.

Perhaps Margaret would know of someone needing a companion, or even a governess to a young child. Mentally she began to work out the sort of salary she might expect, and how long it would take her to save enough for her passage.

As a chambermaid she could expect tips, and though the work might be harder, she could, if she lived frugally, perhaps save enough to buy her passage by the following summer.

As a companion, she would be expected to purchase more suitable clothes, and have all sorts of small expenses to maintain her position. She knew of old how these small purchases added up in no time to a large sum, so she would be able to save almost nothing. It would have to be a chambermaid.

Preoccupied, she talked little, content to listen to Sophia's chatter and Margaret's gossip about their neighbours. Neither of them mentioned Alastair, and Janet wondered where he was, but did not like to ask. Probably he, along with Gordon, Margaret's husband, had gone to lunch in a coffee house.

When it was time to dress for dinner, a simple one just for the family, Margaret reassured her, Janet went upstairs. She had no gown into which she could change, but she could tidy her hair and wash her face. In her room, however, she found Jeannie with a silk gown in a delicious shade of dove grey.

'Mistress gave me this for you, and I've been taking in the waist. You're thinner than she is. I hope I've done it properly. I measured it against the gown you were wearing yesterday, and I think it will fit you,' Jeannie said, some excitement in her voice.

'How kind of your mistress and you, Jeannie. It's a beautiful colour.'

'Mistress says you ought to be wearing black, but she hasn't anything that would fit you, and this is the best she can do.'

'It's very kind of her.'

'It doesn't suit her,' Jeannie confided. 'She has such dark eyes. She lent you a shawl, too.'

Soon Janet was ready, and felt odd in her finery. It was so long since she'd worn such gowns.

It was plain, but beautifully cut, and she took out her grandmother's cairngorms to wear with it. A stranger might take her for a lady, except for her skin, browned by the sun. Sophia would always wear a sunhat, she thought, to preserve her complexion, and probably sleep with some sort of cream on her face, too.

It was only the family for dinner, for which Janet was thankful. She did not feel ready, yet, for facing the curious eyes of the world, or returning to the sort of social engagements she had once enjoyed with her parents in Edinburgh.

Sophia, with whom she had sat all day, was different. Janet found her a delightful companion, and her earlier air of lethargy, the languid pose in which Janet had first seen her, had vanished when she found a companion of her own age to entertain and be entertained by.

It was Alastair who seemed the strangest of them all, Janet found to her surprise. He wore pantaloons and a superbly-cut coat of blue, a paler blue embroidered waistcoat, and his cravat was tied in an intricate fashion. Until now, she had only seen him in riding dress, and though his coat and breeches had been of the finest quality, they had not been so conspicuous by their excellent cut as were his evening clothes.

He was alone in the drawing-room, and strode across to greet her as she entered, leading her to sit beside him on one of the sofas.

'How do you feel? Better, I hope.'

'Thank you, yes,' she replied, feeling almost shy in his company now, 'and I did not have time to thank you for escorting me, bringing me here. I will see about finding a position tomorrow, though. I don't wish to be a burden on your friends for too long.'

'You are no burden. They want to help, and as for this ridiculous notion

Sophia tells me you have taken into your head, you must forget it. I have said I will look after you.'

Margaret came in then, and there was time for no more conversation. At dinner, the food was delicious, the talk entertaining, since Gordon and Margaret swiftly changed the subject if there was any mention of the Highlands, or lairds, sheep or soldiers. Janet found no opportunity to think about her own plans.

She found that opportunity when Jeannie, her mouth pursed in disapproval, brought her a note the next morning, when she came in with the breakfast tray.

'It was handed in at the stables, miss. I don't know why they could not come to the front door with it.'

Janet did not hear. She was busy unfolding the screw of paper and reading the short note.

Come and meet me in an hour outside the back gate. I have a job and there is one for you, too. Murdo.

'How long ago was this handed in, Jeannie? Do you know?'

'Only a few minutes. Tom, one of the grooms, brought it straight up to the house.'

'Thank you.'

Janet thought rapidly as she ate the thin slices of bread and butter, and drank her chocolate. Margaret would want to know where she was going, and might even insist on Jeannie accompanying her, but if she walked in the gardens, surely she'd be able to find the back gate and slip out for a few minutes.

If Murdo really did know of a possible position for her she would think of some scheme to get away from the house while she went to ask for an interview.

She dressed hurriedly. If she went out now, before Margaret and Sophie would have come downstairs, she could evade them for long enough. The gardens, which she could see from her own window, were new, but they had already been designed with many pergolas and arches and similar features which would help to screen her, even though the plants had not yet grown large or luxuriant.

Downstairs, she saw no-one apart from a parlour maid coming from the dining-room. Without curiosity, the girl directed her to a side door which led through a boot room and into the garden. Janet tried not to look as though she were in a hurry, but headed straight for the nearest archway, turning aside once she was through it, and wending her way towards the wall at the back of the property, trying to keep out of view of the house as much as possible.

The gate was locked but to her relief the key was still in the lock, and it turned noiselessly. She slipped through. It was far too early, no more than half an hour had elapsed since she received the note, but Murdo was there, lounging against the wall, chewing a blade of grass.

He sprang upright and came towards her. He was still limping slightly, she noticed, but less than before. He grinned, taking both her hands in his and drawing her close. As he bent to kiss her she pulled away, looking anxiously about her, and he laughed a little at what he thought was her modesty.

'Janet, thank goodness! I thought that supercilious fellow in the stables would probably throw my note away.'

'He didn't, as you see. You have a position? That was quick. Tell me, what is it, and where?'

'At one of the big hotels, as an ostler, and they are looking for chambermaids, so if you go quickly you could obtain a position, too. It's to live in, so we have no problem with finding lodgings, and as soon as we have found our way about we can be wed.'

Janet suppressed a sigh. Would he never give up?

'I need to earn some money, Murdo, and I'm grateful to you, but I won't work in the same hotel unless you understand that I have no intention of marrying you. I'm going to Canada. I need the money for my passage,' she said determinedly.

He began to protest, and Janet turned away. As she lifted her hand to the gate, Murdo seized her arm in a fierce grip that made her wince and swung her round to face him.

'Very well, Janet, if that's how you want it. I won't ask you again. You want better than me, no doubt, with your own fine ways. I can't give you what an English gentleman can,' he added bitterly.

'I don't want that either! Why can't you understand I need to work for myself, not be dependant on a man? Now, please let me go. You're hurting my arm.'

'I'm sorry,' he said, his tone morose. 'Well, if you mean that, and you're not going to become my fine Mr Fenton's doxy, come and take a menial job like the rest of us have to!'

Janet turned on him in fury.

'I never had any intention of becoming any man's doxy, and you're insulting me to even suggest it, Murdo Mackay!'

He ignored her anger.

'Can you come straight away to see the housekeeper?'

'No. I can't leave here without telling Mistress MacBeith, that would be unpardonable. But I'll go as soon as I can. Where is it?'

He gave her directions, and then they parted. Janet was thankful to have the prospect of a job so quickly, but she wondered if Murdo would be able to keep his promise. Ought she to risk working so close to him? But the opportunity was too good to miss, and if she did not take advantage of it, it might be weeks before she had another such chance, and she could deal with Murdo.

She slipped back inside the house without being seen, and went up to her room. She had to devise a way of getting to the hotel, and in the end she decided there was nothing for it but to confide in Margaret.

She found her in the boudoir, and without saying she had met Murdo, just that he had sent her a note, she begged permission to go and apply for the job.

'What's this Murdo to you' Margaret asked bluntly.

'No more than a clansman, a cousin. He wants to marry me, and he's taken that stupid notion into his head, but all I want is to get to Canada, and with my own money,' she added swiftly.

She had no desire to be beholden to either Margaret or Alastair. Margaret looked at her for a long minute, then nodded.

'Very well, if that's what you really want. Let me see, you need some small items, so we will take the carriage and go shopping. Sophia will be content to stay at home and entertain Alastair. Can you be ready in ten minutes?'

'Yes, of course, and thank you so much!'

Margaret had already rung the bell for her maid.

'Off you go then. Ask Jeannie for one of my hats and she'll also find you some gloves.'

Janet sped to her room and ten minutes later was stepping decorously into the town carriage that Margaret had ordered.

A short while later, near the Tolbooth, Margaret halted the carriage and let her alight.

'Do you know the way? Are you sure? Then I'll meet you back here in an hour. Good luck.'

Janet smiled at her tremulously. This wasn't how she'd envisaged being in Glasgow. She had come with the intention of spending a week or so while she found a ship, in relative comfort at a decent inn. Now she would exchange the much greater comfort of the Gordon house for a garret, probably shared with other maids, and hard, unrelenting work in a hotel for a year if she was fortunate, longer if it proved harder to save than she expected.

And all the time, she suspected, she would have to fend off Murdo's unwelcome pleadings.

On thinking about it, she doubted if he would even attempt to keep his promise once they were working in the same establishment and he thought she was more likely to heed him. She sighed and shrugged. She could handle his importunities, and perhaps, she grinned at the thought, there would be other maids who would attract him, be more receptive of his advances, make him forget her. He was, after all, handsome, big and strong.

Many of the girls in the glen would have welcomed his attentions, and she had a suspicion that he had enjoyed flirtations with more than one of them before, or even during the time he had been protesting devotion to her.

The housekeeper at the hotel was able to see her, and subjected her to searching questions about her experience.

When Janet said she wanted to save for her passage to Canada, to join her brother, the woman sniffed.

'Ye'll not save enough for a good while,' she warned. 'But I need maids quickly, and too many of them are flighty pieces who move on when it suits them, no consideration for my inconvenience. Can you come here tonight, and be ready to start in the morning?'

Janet took a deep breath and nodded. 'Yes.'

If it were that easy to change jobs, she was thinking, it was what she would do if Murdo became a nuisance. Working here, she would hear of other openings.

'I will bring my things here tonight,' she said.

The housekeeper nodded.

'Let me show you the room you'll have, then you can go straight there and settle in.'

She took Janet up to a small room at the top and back of the building, where half a dozen pallets were squeezed in with barely room to step between them.

'That will be yours, farthest from the window. And there's a peg for each of you, for your clothes.'

Janet peered through the gloom at the tiny slit which was the window, fast closed, and the glass filthy, and suppressed a sigh. The air would be foetid up here under the roof, especially when it was hot, but she could see no way of opening the window, and fully expected the other maids to protest if she even suggested it. Town-bred girls, she had discovered, disliked and distrusted fresh air.

Margaret MacBeith was waiting for her at the Tolbooth as arranged and she scrambled swiftly into the carriage. This would be her last ride in anything so comfortable.

'Well, did you obtain the position?'

Janet grinned at her.

'Yes, and I go there tonight. Thank

you so much, Margaret, for helping me. It would have been difficult without you.'

'What will Alastair say when he knows?'

Janet sighed.

'I imagine he'll be angry. Men don't like to be thwarted, and he was determined to rule my life. Oh, I'm grateful to him, I don't mean I'm not, and to you, but I can't depend on either of you. Why, I didn't even know him a month ago! And he has no cause to be responsible for me.'

She fell silent, musing over how much her life had changed, and Margaret sat and watched her, also silent. Janet was thinking back to the carefree days in the glen, Mary's death, and the horrors of the long journey to Glasgow.

She was secretly a little relieved that she did not have to set out on another, longer and more hazardous journey for a while, little though she expected to enjoy the work at the hotel. But there was no help for it, and she would be an excellent chambermaid and earn big tips so that her hoard of money would increase rapidly.

She came to with a start when the carriage stopped and the steps were let down outside the MacBeith house.

'I will pack my bundle and slip away as soon as possible,' she said hurriedly to Margaret. 'I really don't want to speak to Alastair. He'd only try to persuade me not to go, and I won't be beholden to him any more, either. Will you tell him I shall be all right? And please don't tell him where to come to find me!'

Margaret made no move to alight from the carriage.

'What about your pony?'

Jane had forgotten that.

'Is he in your stables? I never gave him a thought! How remiss of me.'

'You have had rather a lot of other things to think about,' Margaret said comfortingly. 'Shall I keep him for you?'

'That would put you to trouble and expense. Oh, dear, please, will you sell him for me?'

'I will, and get the money to you somehow. It will be a start towards your Canada fund.'

Impulsively, Janet hugged her.

'You have been a real friend, and I do thank you so much.'

'I wonder if you will when you have been slaving away for a month or two cleaning rooms and making beds, and carrying coals and slops up endless stairs?' she asked, and Janet laughed a little ruefully.

'I'm strong. I worked hard from morn to night in Strathnaver. I'm no weakling, and I have an important reason for doing it. Next summer, I hope, I'll be off to Nova Scotia.'

'Come and see me occasionally, please, and don't dare leave without telling me.'

'I won't, I promise.'

7

For the first few days at the hotel, Janet was too weary to do more than fall into bed at night and go straight to sleep. She had no time or energy to mourn for Mary, or think of Alastair. On her first half day off, when she wanted nothing better than to crawl into her bed and rest, she found Murdo waiting for her at the foot of the stairs to the attics.

'I arranged to have the same time off as you,' he said, and Janet thought he had an intolerably smug look in his eyes.

How could she ever have imagined she liked him, she asked herself.

'Yes?' was all she could manage.

'We can go out, see a bit of Glasgow together,' he suggested.

'I'm too tired,' she replied, beginning to climb the stairs. 'All I really need is my bed.'

For one appalled moment, as he placed a foot on the step behind her, she thought he was about to suggest that he kept her company, but then he laughed.

'It's too hard work for you, is it? You'd prefer to be a lady of leisure, kept by that strutting Englishman? Are you going out with him? Is that why you don't want me? Well, I've had enough, Janet Mackay! Don't come crawling back to me for comfort when he's left you. You have to choose, me or him, and this is the last chance I'm giving you.'

'I've never wanted either of you,' Janet flared, 'and it's about time you accepted it, Murdo.'

She stared at him until his own gaze dropped, and he turned away.

'Janet, you've been bewitched!' she heard him mutter.

Wearily, she climbed the stairs and sank on to her lumpy, straw pallet. Normally the lumps did not keep her awake, she was too exhausted and would have slept happily on the bare, wooden floor. Perhaps it was because it was the middle of the day that she could not settle, and felt every unevenness sticking into her ribs and hips and legs, making it impossible to sleep as she'd hoped.

When another of the maids came upstairs and seemed eager to talk, Janet welcomed the distraction. Betty was a cheerful, uncomplicated girl who had done her best to be friendly and show Janet how she could do things properly but with the least effort.

'He's here again,' she said, 'asking for you.'

'Murdo?' Janet asked, surprised.

She'd thought he had at last accepted her rejection.

'No, not him! I know he's been making sheep's eyes at you all the time you've worked here, but he doesn't drive a smart phaeton, with high-bred horses and a groom in livery. Not unless he's stolen them!' she giggled.

'Then who do you mean?' Janet demanded.

'Some Englishman. He's been asking about you for days, and someone told him you have this afternoon off. He's sent a note. Here it is.'

She handed over a sheet of paper, sealed, Janet saw, with a brief moment of thankfulness. Many of the maids had been to school for at least a year or two, and could read a little. If, as she feared, this was from Alastair, for what other Englishman did she know, she did not want the other maids to gossip about her more than they already would.

She opened it slowly, and read the short message inside.

I have a letter for you, from your brother. Please will you come down and speak with me for a few minutes? I will wait at the back of the hotel. Alastair Fenton.

Janet's weariness vanished, and she sprang up and began to change into her best gown, and brush her hair. Betty chuckled.

'I've heard he's a right handsome fellow,' she said with a wink.

'He has a letter from my brother, my brother who's gone to Canada,' Janet explained.

'Then why has he been here several times this week? He could have left the letter for you. My Duncan would have given it to you.'

Janet scarcely listened, though she wondered the same. Duncan was one of the porters, and Betty learned all sorts of gossip from him.

'Well, I'd best be getting back or the old hag will be after me,' Betty said with a sigh.

Janet chuckled. The housekeeper was a handsome, middle-aged woman, but she was stern, and the maids all called her the old hag. Janet suspected she knew this, but didn't care so long as they did their work satisfactorily.

She was ready moments later, and went down the stairs, not aware that her step was now sprightly, and her eyes bright with eagerness. All trace of weariness had gone, and she could hardly wait, eager to read what her brother had written. At the back of the hotel she found Alastair sitting in a phaeton. It probably belonged to Gordon, she thought, as would the horses and the tiny groom who was standing at the heads of the horses.

Alastair leaped down, smiling at her in a way that made her blush with embarrassment in case any of the other maids saw her, and handed her up into the vehicle. He climbed back into it, and nodded to the groom, who turned and walked away as Alastair shook the reins and put the horses to a gentle trot.

'My letter? It's true, isn't it? How did you get it?' Janet demanded breathlessly.

'It's true, but let's go somewhere quieter before you read it. I had worried that Iain might have written to you in Strathnaver, so I asked one of the ministers to send it on to me if a letter came. I didn't expect it to be so soon, though.'

'How did you know where I was working?'

'Margaret told me when she knew about the letter. She hopes you'll forgive her for breaking her promise.'

He guided the horse through the traffic and Janet had to contain her impatience until he drew to a halt on Glasgow Green, the vast, open space beside the River Clyde which was a pleasure ground for the whole of the citizenry.

Janet almost snatched the letter when he held it out to her, and tore off the covering impatiently. She began to read, pausing occasionally to reread some of Iain's cramped handwriting. Then, looking blank, she raised her head and stared in front of her, not speaking. Alastair, with a murmured word of comfort, put his hand on top of hers, and she turned to him.

'He's married,' she said. 'He's married a girl he met on the ship.'

'It's to be expected. A young man facing a new life in a strange country, he wouldn't wish to be alone. Do you mind?'

Janet shook her head fiercely.

'No, of course not, if he's happy, but he was so in love with Elizabeth Ross, and devastated when she was killed. Her family had a town house near ours in Edinburgh, and they'd known one another for years, and it had never been anyone else for Iain. How could he change his affections so suddenly?'

'He and this girl would have been together for six weeks or more on the ship, remember. That's plenty of time to come to know someone. And perhaps he had to decide quickly, before they lost sight of one another if her family was going to a different place.'

'But he loved Elizabeth so much.'

'She was lost to him, Janet. I'm not saying this girl is second best. I believe it's possible to love more than once, and what's more, to know in an instant if someone is the right person for you. What does he say about her?'

'She came from somewhere near Oban, and her parents and small brother died on the voyage.'

'What is it you're afraid of? That he won't want you now? Being married doesn't cut men off from other family ties.'

'No, but things are bound to be different. They have to be. There were only the two of us left. And, oh, Alastair, her name's Mary. I would have to call her, think of her, as Mary!'

'That would hurt, being your grand-mother's name?'

Janet took a deep, shuddering breath.

'I'll get used to it, in time. I expect I'll be used to it before I even leave Glasgow. It will be strange, but lots of girls have the same name. Mary is a very common name, after all.'

'You don't have to go,' he said gently.

'Marry Murdo, you mean?' Janet laughed. 'I never would, and I think I have convinced him at last. No, I still mean to go, and I'll have time to get used to the idea of Iain being wed. I should have thought of it months ago. He was bound to marry eventually, but somehow I never thought of it, not so soon after Elizabeth.'

'Not Murdo,' Alastair went on quietly. 'He would never do for you. I'm asking you to marry me.'

Janet turned and stared at him in amazement.

'Marry you? But I thought . . . '

She broke off. It was too embarrassing to tell him that she had imagined should he ever want her, it would not be through marriage.

'You thought what?' he prompted.

She shook her head. Neither could she tell him she thought he would marry Sophia, now his brother was dead. If it had been a suitable match for his brother, for reasons of uniting their estates, it would be a suitable one now for him.

'I didn't think you could want to marry me. I don't have big estates, or any sort of fortune.'

'I see. Are those really important, the

only reasons you can think of for marriage?'

Janet flushed painfully.

'I think you have offered out of pity, and that I could not endure. Please will you take me back now? I am very tired, and was hoping to rest this afternoon.'

'Very well, but only if you promise to come out with me again, and tell me how things go with you, and if you wish to go to Canada immediately,' he said, 'I will lend you the money in that case.'

He refused to start the carriage until she agreed reluctantly, and they arranged to meet at the same time the following week.

'By then you will have been able to absorb the news,' he said lightly, 'and know better what you wish to do.'

Janet spent the rest of the day lying on her bed, unable to sleep, trying to decide what Alastair had meant. The news he'd referred to must be Iain's marriage, but did he mean this when he talked about her decisions? Could he have meant that astounding offer of marriage?

She admitted to herself, reluctantly, that she was tempted by the notion, now that it had been suggested. From their first meeting he had made such an impact on her that he was rarely out of her thoughts. He was exciting, his kisses made her tremble. Was that love?

She wasn't sure she knew what love was. She'd believed it was because he was so different from the clansmen, or any of the men she'd met in Edinburgh in her earlier life, that she thought so much about him. Did she, incredible though it might seem, love him, a wealthy Englishman? Even more unbelievable was the possibility that he might love her.

Yet love was no basis for marriage, not for people like Alastair Fenton. From the little she had seen and heard while staying with the MacBeiths, she had understood Alastair's estates were extensive and profitable. He had to marry someone who could bring him more wealth, or land, or influence, or social elevation. Men like him never married penniless girls from Highland crofts.

She hadn't always been penniless, she reminded herself. Her father had been a respected businessman, her mother from a good Edinburgh family. If they had not died she could have expected, in time, to marry well, even if she would not have considered looking as high as Alastair.

Janet sighed and tried to forget it all and think about Iain. She hoped he would be happy and tried to be thankful that he would have the comfort of a wife in his new, probably harsh and difficult life. Should she travel to Canada now? He had been insistent in his letter that he and Mary were eagerly awaiting her coming, though of course they did not know of her grandmother's death. But they had all known Mary could not live for much longer, so it was natural Iain should refer to the time when she would be free.

She could be an embarrassment if she went too soon. How could any newly-wed couple welcome a third person? She'd heard tales of how the new settlers had built small, one-room, log cabins, even less spacious than the Highland crofts. Iain and his bride might be confined to one room to begin with, and that would never do. Even if she went next summer, it would be too soon. But she doubted her ability to survive more than a year of the already excruciating boredom of this job. It would have made life so much simpler if she could have believed Alastair really wanted her. She admitted that the thought of marriage to him, never before dreamed of, because it would have seemed too impossible, was tempting.

Did she love him? Her thoughts went round and round, and she tossed restlessly. Even if she did love him, and he felt more than pity for her, it would be wrong to give in to the temptation.

There was Sophia. In every way she would be the ideal wife for him. If she had been unpleasant in any way Janet could have persuaded herself she would have made Alastair miserable, and she might have been prepared to save him from such a fate.

At the thought she laughed out loud. Such a sacrifice was ludicrous. Besides, Sophia was pretty, a delightful companion, anxious to please and friendly. She would make Alastair happy as well as bring him lands to add to his own. Janet sat up and punched her lumpy pillow. She ought to be pleased for him. The fact was she was horribly confused, and didn't know what she wanted. Was it to be Canada and becoming an unwelcome third in Iain's household, or ignoring all commonsense would she accept Alastair's proposal?

No, she could tolerate neither situation. There had to be a third way out of this dilemma. For a brief, very brief second she thought of Murdo, but as hurriedly dismissed him. She could never marry him. Her problems unresolved, she eventually fell asleep, to wake heavy-eyed and drag herself about her duties the following day.

Matters were not helped when Murdo cornered her in the stableyard when she was sent on an errand to one of the visiting grooms.

'I saw you yesterday, riding with that damned Englishman when you'd told me you were too weary to go out with me!' he stormed at her, pinning her against the wall with his hands placed either side of her head.

'I had a message,' she began, but he interrupted furiously.

'A message from him sends you hurrying to his side, whereas I have to plead for you to even give me the time of day! Janet, I love you, I want to marry you, I'll do anything for you.'

She felt trapped. How could she keep on disappointing him when he was so obviously unhappy at her continued rejection, unlike Alastair, she thought. He had accepted her refusal calmly, and did not appear too downcast about it, even offering to help her get to Canada. He couldn't feel anything for her, not like poor Murdo did.

'I might consider it,' she said at last.

Perhaps that would satisfy him, and prevent this constant pleading. She might be able to bargain with him, and gradually make him realise that it would not do.

'Janet, ye mean it?'

To her annoyance, he lifted her off her feet and swung her round in an excess of joy, and then pulled her to him and gave her a long kiss. She submitted for a moment, and then pulled away. It wasn't like Alastair's kisses, and this was no way to deter him. She must have been mad to give him any encouragement.

Murdo was still talking, and she forced herself to listen.

'What did you say?' she asked. 'What's that about rooms to live in?'

'Well, we couldn't live here. They don't have rooms for married couples,

145

but one of us could get a job at another hotel, and if we lived out they would pay us more. I have already spoken for some rooms, and paid rent for a year. Janet, it would be wonderful!'

'Where did you find money for a year's rent?' she asked.

The clansmen never had much to spare, and Murdo had been trying to run his family's holding alone for the past two years. He grinned in triumph.

'Your passage money,' he said. 'I took it while you were by the river, the night Mary died. I decided it was safer for me to look after it than leave it in an unlocked box anyone could have opened. I thought you'd discover it was gone earlier.'

Janet felt as though she'd been kicked in the stomach. She felt sick, with an anger more cold and deadly than she had ever felt before.

'You stole my money?' she breathed at last. 'And you let me think it had gone for ever?'

'I had to stop you going to Canada,'

he explained, without any apparent realisation of the enormity of what he'd done.

'When you knew how desperate I was to get there? You stole it, and you've condemned me to slave away in this place for a pittance when I could have been on the sea by now, on my way to Iain?'

'But I don't want you to leave me! I want us to get married, and I have a home ready for us.'

Janet suddenly exploded with anger.

'You don't love me, Murdo Mackay! All you care about is what you want. This finishes us. I'll never marry you, and if you don't get that money back for me I'll charge you with theft, and you'll be put in prison, and I hope you'll rot there!'

8

Janet, exhausted by the strength of her fury, didn't sleep at all that night. Her first instinct, when she had pushed the bewildered, protesting Murdo away from her and flown up the stairs to her room, had been to find Alastair and beg him to help.

Then calmer thoughts prevailed. How could she demand his help? This was something she had to deal with herself.

She was too busy and too weary to do much more than drag herself through her work the following day. She still felt too sick to eat, so in the scant twenty minutes she was allowed for her own dinner, she went out to the stables and demanded of an astonished groom that he fetch Murdo to speak with her.

Murdo, looking wary, appeared from one of the stalls where he had been grooming a horse.

'Janet?' he asked cautiously.

She controlled her anger and tried to speak calmly.

'If you can somehow get the rent returned, I will not set the constable on you.'

'But how can I do that? They won't give it back to me.'

'Then you must find someone else to rent the rooms, who will give you the money,' she snapped.

Why was he so helpless? How could she ever have had even the slightest liking for him?

'How can I do that?' he muttered dourly.

Janet gritted her teeth.

'If you love me as you say, you'll manage it. But just in case, give me the address of where these rooms are. I will go and ask for the money back, and tell them why.'

'No, Janet, don't do that. I'll try, I really will.'

'The address, tell me, and I'll give

you two days to do something about the whole thing.'

It might still be possible for her to arrange a passage to Canada, she was thinking, if only she could get her money back.

The thought did not excite her as much as it would have done a few days earlier.

Reluctantly Murdo gave her directions to one of the small, older houses close to Glasgow Cathedral.

'But please don't go,' he begged her. 'I'll try to get the money back, I promise.'

'Two days, starting this afternoon.'

She swung round and went back indoors, her momentary burst of energy leaving her. By the evening, she could have screamed with tiredness.

The following day it was not much better. She felt faint with hunger but still could not eat more than a mouthful of bread. A night spent fretting about if Murdo would be able to restore her money left her limp and miserable.

Added to this was the indecision of whether or not she really did want to go to Canada and join Iain and his bride, possibly complicating their lives if they felt they had to welcome and look after her.

At dinner time, when she hoped Murdo would be there to return her money, she went out to the stables.

'Where's Murdo Mackay?' she asked.

'He left right after ye tore into 'im. Never seen a grown man so badly shook up,' a grinning groom told her.

'Did he say where he was going?'

'Muttered somethin' about which devil was worst,' he said, and sniggered.

So he had deserted her! This had been at the back of her mind all along, contributing to her unease. Had he, finally understanding that she would never marry him, simply retrieved the money he'd stolen, taken it and departed, or, being unable to do so, been unable to face her?

It was up to her to make the attempt. Not caring about her work, she went straight to the address he'd given her and hammered on the shabby-looking door. Had Murdo really expected her to be pleased at the thought of living here with him?

'Hold your horses! Don't knock the door down,' a woman's querulous voice said.

It would not take much to do that, Janet thought in disgust.

A thin, almost scrawny, woman opened the door.

'Have you seen Murdo Mackay?' Janet asked brusquely. 'He used money he stole from me to pay you a year's rent, I understand.'

The woman frowned.

'That's as may be. It's none o' my business.'

'Has he been here?'

'Aye, this very morning, and I gave him the gold, less enough to compensate me for my trouble, of course,' she whined.

Janet wasn't sure if she could believe her, but there was no more she could do. If Murdo had left, the money was gone for ever. She knew now that she should have insisted on coming here with him, but she had been in such a state of fury she hadn't been thinking straight. She thanked the woman and turned away. She could only return to the hotel and wait, wondering what had delayed him, making frantic plans also to search for him if he did not appear.

★ ★ ★

Wearily she resumed her tasks, and the stairs seemed twice as steep, the trays much heavier, than before. By the time everything was done she was barely able to drag herself up the stairs, but she still had to take a can of hot water for a newly-arrived guest in one of the best front bedrooms.

'Well, you're a welcome sight for a weary traveller,' a young man said as she pushed open the door. 'I didn't expect to find a girl as pretty as you in this dull place. Come in, put that down, and let me have a really good look at you.'

Janet glared at him as she walked over to the washstand. She could normally turn aside these pleasantries, the attempts by men on their own to flirt with her, but tonight she had not the patience.

'Your hot water, sir,' she said curtly.

'Oh, come, don't be cross with me. I'm sure you'd like to earn a little more, for keeping me company. We could have such fun.'

He had come up behind her, and Janet felt his hand resting on her hip. She gave him a fierce shove with her elbow, and as he staggered back, wincing, she raised the can and poured the hot water over his head, then for good measure threw the can to the floor and slapped him on the face as hard as she could, and stalked from the room.

He complained, of course, but not until the following morning, when he was departing. Janet was called to see the manager.

'This is unacceptable behaviour,' he told her pompously.

Janet glared at him. This was too much, to be blamed for a guest's lewd suggestions.

'I am employed to carry coals and trays and hot water, and make the beds, not sleep in them with guests who feel the need for the services of a common drab,' she snapped.

'You are employed to do your work,' he said, sniffing, 'which does not include being impertinent to guests, and, what is more, assaulting them. Besides, you were absent yesterday for an hour without explanation. You will take your belongings and leave at once.'

'I'd be happy to, when you have paid me the money I have earned so far,' Janet said, quietly furious.

'You have forfeited any money.'

'Then I shall go and stand outside your hotel and tell all your guests how you treat your staff.'

They haggled, but eventually Janet won her point and the manager reluctantly handed over the few coins due to her. She looked at them ruefully. They would scarcely pay for the journey down to the docks, let alone across the Atlantic.

Buoyed up with her anger, Janet stormed to her miserable room and packed her few belongings in a shawl, then marched out of the front door of the hotel, ignoring the sneer on the porter's face. He clearly knew why she was leaving.

Only when she was outside did it occur to her that, should Murdo by some miracle return, he would not be able to find her.

She looked round, dazed, and her gaze caught a flash of bright green. It was a child, little more than a toddler, staggering out into the roadway, and beyond her was a coach, pulled by a team of powerful-looking horses, bearing down relentlessly.

Flinging aside her bundle, Janet swooped down on the child, grabbed her and flung her aside, but before she could scramble to safety herself she felt a vicious blow on the head and knew no more.

She came round lying on a bench inside the coffee room of the hotel, with Sophia's anxious face bent over her.

'Oh, thank God! We thought you'd never regain your senses. Janet, how do you feel?'

'Sophia? What — why are you here? Oh! I remember, the little girl! Is she safe?'

Janet shivered. She could see it all once more, the horses about to trample the child, but it was all so slow this time, she knew she'd be too afraid to do it again.

'Apart from a grazed arm when she fell after you'd thrown her to safety, she's fine. Her nursemaid was hysterical, and we've sent her home. We, Alastair and I, were driving behind the coach and saw it happen. You were so brave! But you, poor Janet, how do you feel?'

Janet tried to sit up, and winced.

'My head aches. Did one of the horses kick me?'

'No. Fortunately, the coachman managed to turn them enough to miss you, but one of the carriage wheels knocked you over, and you've been senseless for ages.'

'Don't exaggerate, my love,' a male voice intervened, and Janet turned her head and saw, standing slightly behind Sophia, a young man dressed in a travelling cloak with innumerable shoulder capes.

Sophia sighed.

'Well, it seemed like hours! Long enough for Hugo to carry you in here. Janet, this is Hugo Buchanan, my fiancé. He arrived here in the coach. We came to meet him, that's why I am here and saw it all. You were incredibly brave!'

Janet wondered if she was still senseless.

'Your fiancé? But I thought Alastair . . .'

'His brother? Oh, that was a long time ago! I was betrothed to James when I was a child. Hugo is Margaret's cousin, and we're to be married soon from her house, and we'll live here in Glasgow.'

'Are you well enough to move?' Hugo asked. 'Alastair has gone to order a carriage to take you back to Margaret's house. Sophia and I have to go to see some old friends, and we are already late.'

'I'm sorry,' Janet began, and Sophia, chiding Hugo for his insensitivity, tried to explain at the same time that they were not late at all.

'Run away and leave her to me,' a voice said from the door, and, looking up as Sophia and Hugo left, Janet's eyes fell on Alastair.

Janet sat up, ignoring the waves of dizziness which swept over her.

'Alastair?'

'Sit still. I've sent someone for a tisane which will help, and then I'll drive you home.'

He sat beside her and put his arm round her shoulders. She relaxed against him.

'My clothes, I dropped them.'

'Don't worry, they're here. But why were you leaving? Surely you haven't arranged a passage so soon?'

'I don't have the money,' she told him tiredly, then blinked.

He was holding out to her the purse of gold coins she'd last seen when she packed it in Strathnaver.

'Yes, you do.'

'You?' she said stupidly. 'But Murdo, he'd spent it.'

'I know. The wretched man came to me and confessed, when the landlady refused to refund him the rent. He was too cowardly to come back and tell you. I went back with him and, shall I say, we persuaded her that it would be rather unfortunate for her if the constables heard about it.'

'Would it?' Janet asked. 'She took it in good faith, even though she was an unpleasant harridan.'

'She believed me enough to repay it. Now, if you still wish it, you can book your passage but I suggest you wait for the next boat.'

'Why?'

'Murdo decided that, if all hope of you had gone, which he seemed to think was the case, he'd rather take my offer to pay his passage and go to Canada. I think he is a little afraid of you,' he added, chuckling. 'He's on the boat which sails tomorrow. I doubt you'd wish to sail with him.'

She certainly would not. It would be highly embarrassing for them both. Janet began to laugh, and then held her head.

'Oh, dear, it aches so!'

At that moment, an anxious-looking manager appeared, carrying a small tray on which was a glass filled with a cloudy liquid. He glanced cautiously at Alastair and offered the glass to Janet.

'This will help, miss,' he said ingratiatingly.

His pomposity had totally disappeared. Alastair seemed to have the ability either to charm or terrify people into doing what he wished. She drank the tisane slowly, and smiled at the manager reassuringly. She had behaved badly, whatever the provocation and he'd been well within his rights to dismiss her. Had Alastair heard about her dismissal, and had he threatened this man, too? Would she be able to get her job back?

Then she berated herself for a fool. She didn't need the job. She had money enough now, thanks to Alastair, to go to Canada. But suddenly she didn't want to go.

'Can you walk?' Alastair asked, and Janet nodded slowly, relieved to find that her head was pounding less violently already.

'I think so,' she said, and stood up, swaying a little and clinging to his arm.

Slowly they walked outside, and Alastair lifted her into the closed carriage which was waiting for them. Leaping in after her, he sat down and held her tightly, protecting her from any jolting as the carriage moved off, and soon she was back in her familiar room at the MacBeiths' house. There, she slept deeply for the first time in several days, and woke refreshed, her aching cleared.

The sun was high in the sky, a brilliant blue sky with no clouds in sight. Jeannie peeped in soon afterwards and asked if she wanted breakfast, and Janet found that she was ravenous.

'Then Mr Alastair wants to see you, about the ship, I think,' Jeannie said as she backed out of the room.

To help her arrange a passage, no doubt, Janet thought, and wished she knew her own mind. Did she want to go or not? If she did not go, what would she do? She certainly would not become a chambermaid again, but she was too confused to think of other possibilities.

After a hearty breakfast, she let Jeannie dress her in the grey silk gown Margaret had lent her before, and brush her hair gently, arranging it in a simple style, tied back by a ribbon. When she was ready she went as

Jeannie told her to Margaret's boudoir. She must thank her for her hospitality as soon as possible.

It was Alastair, however, who awaited her, looking more handsome than ever. He smiled and came towards her to take her hand and draw her to sit on a chair beside the window.

'How do you feel?'

'Much better, thank you,' she said, and wondered why her voice quavered.

'Well enough to discuss what we do now?'

'Yes,' she said, her heart sinking.

He was doubtless anxious to send her on her way. Maybe he had even found another ship ready to sail. Suddenly she knew that she did not wish to leave Scotland, not even to rejoin Iain. Or rather, she amended, she wanted to be near Alastair, whether that was in Scotland or England. The very thought of saying farewell, of never seeing him again, was torture. She hadn't the slightest idea, though, of how this was to be achieved.

'You have the choice,' he said, and his voice sounded odd.

He stood up and began to pace the small room, turning impatiently every few steps when he was impeded by the furniture.

'You can afford to go to Canada, or you can accept my offer of looking after you. I believe,' he went on, smiling slightly, 'that your reluctance previously was partly because you thought I would be marrying Sophia. As you can see, that is not so. Her betrothal to my brother was an arranged match, and she felt free, this time, to wed someone she really loved. Not that I would ever have asked her, for delightful though she is, I don't love her, nor she me. I have this odd notion of not wanting to marry when I cannot love, too.'

Janet had nothing to say. A crazy, wild seed of hope lay somewhere in the region of her heart, which was beating erratically. She'd not known it before, or not been willing to admit it to herself, because it seemed hopeless, but now she knew with utter certainty that she loved Alastair. It was a strange feeling, not at all like the love she'd had for Mary. It was somehow wilder and warmer.

Then she came down to earth. She was misunderstanding him. She must be.

'Well?' he asked. 'Will you marry me, Janet?'

'It's not possible. I'm not your sort of girl. I'm poor. You found me in a Highland croft.'

Suddenly he was kneeling in front of her, and had captured her hands gently in his.

'Janet, my love, you have a purse of gold. I have seen it for myself. You are rich enough to buy some silk gowns, but I'd take you without them, and I mean to give you many more. Sweetheart, I loved you from the moment I saw you on that hillside. You can't believe I go round kissing every pretty girl I meet, surely?'

He was laughing, his head on a level

with hers, and as he bent towards her, his lips coming nearer, agonisingly slowly, Janet began to believe that he meant what he said. Tentatively she raised her arms, and as he clasped her to him, she flung them round his neck, laughing herself.

'Oh, Alastair, I love you, too! I didn't know, but it has always been so much better when you were with me, and I don't want to go to Canada. I want to marry you!'

She was breathless from his kisses, incoherent with happiness, wanting only to be with him, to have him kiss and caress her as he was doing, for the rest of her life.

'We'll marry here as soon as we can, and then I'll take you home. Will you mind living in England? We can come back as often as you like.'

'I don't mind where I am if I'm with you.'

Much later, Margaret peeped into the room, then backed out hastily, pushing Sophia aside. They smiled at one another and tiptoed away.

We do hope that you have enjoyed reading this large print book.

Did you know that all of our titles are available for purchase?

We publish a wide range of high quality large print books including:
Romances, Mysteries, Classics
General Fiction
Non Fiction and Westerns

Special interest titles available in large print are:
The Little Oxford Dictionary
Music Book, Song Book
Hymn Book, Service Book

Also available from us courtesy of Oxford University Press:
Young Readers' Dictionary
(large print edition)
Young Readers' Thesaurus
(large print edition)

For further information or a free brochure, please contact us at:
Ulverscroft Large Print Books Ltd.,
The Green, Bradgate Road, Anstey,
Leicester, LE7 7FU, England.
Tel: (00 44) **0116 236 4325**
Fax: (00 44) **0116 234 0205**

Other titles in the
Linford Romance Library:

TO BE WITH YOU

Audrey Weigh

Heather, the proud owner of a small bus line, loves the countryside in her corner of Tasmania. Her life begins to change when two new men move into the area. Colin's charm overcomes her first resistance, while Grant also proves a warmer person than expected. But Colin is jealous when Grant gains special attention. The final test comes with the prospect of living in Hobart. Could Heather bear to leave her home and her business to be with the man she loves?

FINGALA, MAID OF RATHAY

Mary Cummins

On his deathbed, Sir James Montgomery of Rathay asks his daughter, Fingala, to swear that she will not honour her marriage contract until her brother Patrick, the new heir, returns from serving the King. Patrick must marry. Rathay must not be left without a mistress. But Patrick has fallen in love with the Lady Catherine Gordon whom the King, James IV, has given in marriage to the young man who claims to be Richard of York, one of the princes in the Tower.